WHAT
COMES
NEXT

ALSO BY ROB BUYEA

THE MR. TERUPT SERIES

Because of Mr. Terupt

Mr. Terupt Falls Again

Saving Mr. Terupt

Goodbye, Mr. Terupt

THE PERFECT SCORE SERIES

The Perfect Score

The Perfect Secret

The Perfect Star

WHAT COMES NEXT

ROB BUYEA

DELACORTE PRESS

All rights reserved. Published in the United States by Delacorte Press, an imprint of Random House Children's Books, a division of Penguin Random House LLC, New York.

Delacorte Press is a registered trademark and the colophon is a trademark of Penguin Random House LLC.

Visit us on the Web! rhcbooks.com

Educators and librarians, for a variety of teaching tools, visit us at RHTeachersLibrarians.com

Library of Congress Cataloging-in-Publication Data
Names: Buyea, Rob, author.
Title: What comes next / Rob Buyea.
Description: First edition. | New York : Delacorte Press, [2021] | Audience: Ages 9–12. | Summary: Twelve-year-old Thea, devastated after seeing her best friend die, begins to open to the possibility of new friendships and forgiveness, and comes to believe in what cannot be fully explained.
Identifiers: LCCN 2020048029 (print) | LCCN 2020048030 (ebook) | ISBN 978-0-525-64802-4 (hardcover) | ISBN 978-0-525-64803-1 (library binding) | ISBN 978-0-525-64804-8 (ebk)
Subjects: CYAC: Grief—Fiction. | Selective mutism—Fiction. | Dogs—Fiction. | Family life—Fiction. | Best friends—Fiction. | Friendship—Fiction.
Classification: LCC PZ7.B98316 Wh 2021 (print) | LCC PZ7.B98316 (ebook) | DDC [Fic]—dc23

The text of this book is set in 12-point Amasis MT.
Interior design by Ken Crossland
Jacket art used under license from Shutterstock.com

Printed in the United States of America
10 9 8 7 6 5 4 3 2 1
First Edition

For my dogs, who've been
loyal writing partners and have
given me many incredible stories to tell

FOREWARNING!

When you own a dog, you end up with lots of incredible tales to tell, but none are quite like the one I've got for you now—not even *Old Yeller* or *Where the Red Fern Grows*. And I know, those are forever classic dog stories. I love them too. But what happened to me is totally different. It's something you've got to hear, and I'll warn you, you're probably not going to believe it, but it's true— every word. I swear on Charlie's grave.

PART I

1

SPARKY

Sparky was our first family dog, but really he was Mom and Dad's dog. They had him well before me, so by the time I was ready to run, good ol' Spark was already beginning to slow down. And by the time my sisters joined us—Livvy first and then Abby—he had slowed down considerably.

Sparky was a faithful companion, as loyal a dog as you'll ever find, so he hung on for quite a while. I remember how he would struggle up our stairs every night so that he could sleep by Dad's bedside—and when I say struggle, I mean struggle. It got to the point where Spark started dribbling pee and dropping turds when he made the climb—it was that bad. That was when Dad started carrying him up the two flights.

It wasn't long after that when we had to say goodbye. I was eight and my sisters were four and three when his time finally came to an end. That was a hard day—but not my worst. Mom and Dad were especially sad, but they smiled through their tears as we stood by Sparky's fresh gravesite and took turns recalling favorite memories of our beloved dog.

"I'll never forget the day Spark grabbed Thea's dirty diaper," Dad mused. "Boy, was it a messy one. And ripe. I must've used thirty wipes trying to clean your butt," he said to me. "Sparky snatched that thing when I wasn't looking. Your mother and I tried, but we couldn't stop him. He streaked past us and raced down the hall."

"And jumped right in the middle of our bed," Mom finished.

My sisters and I giggled. It didn't matter that we'd heard that one a hundred times before. The poopy-diaper-makes-poopy-bed story was a classic in our house.

"Or how about the time he got into the closet and scarfed down all the Halloween candy I had hidden," Mom continued.

Dad groaned. "He's lucky it didn't kill him. You can still see the stain on our living room carpet from the chocolate mud puddle that dummyhead threw up. It just poured out of him."

"Yucky," Abby said.

Mom and Dad shook their heads and laughed. My sisters didn't know any better, so those funny stories had them asking for another puppy before we'd even finished putting Sparky to rest. Silently, I was hoping for the same thing, so I didn't shush them.

It took a while—almost four years to be exact, and a lot had happened and changed by then—but eventually we got our wish. Only problem was, I didn't care anymore. After something terrible happens, you stop caring about dogs and everything else.

2

MY FIRST FISH

I was better at observing and sketching and writing in my journal, but I gave in to Charlie's persistent requests and held his fishing pole like he'd shown me, line in my left hand and rod in my right.

"Now pull back and let it rip," Charlie said, stepping out of the way.

I think he was more excited than me—his best friend was finally giving this a try. I did what he said, but when I threw it forward nothing happened. My line didn't go anywhere.

"Tree fish!" Charlie cheered.

I turned and looked. My lure had caught on a leaf behind me. "Ugh," I groaned.

"Don't worry. It happens to the best of us," Charlie said, walking over and getting it unhooked for me. "Reel up the slack and give it another try, but watch out for the trees," he teased.

"You could've warned me about that the first time."

"Yeah, yeah. Just be careful. That's one of my best spinners you're using."

I set my feet, took aim, and let it rip. My line flew out over the creek and fell into the water.

"Good," Charlie exclaimed. "Now reel. That's what makes the spinner do its thing. Nice and easy. And don't stop."

I kept reeling, silently hoping, barely breathing, until I had the lure back in. "Nothing," I grumbled.

"That's all right. Do it again," Charlie said. "If you can get your lure to land closer to those rocks, you'll get a fish."

"How do you know?" I challenged. I may have asked that question, but only because I was growing frustrated and not because I doubted Charlie. He was amazing at fishing. I'd seen him catch hundreds.

"I told you, that's one of my best lures," he replied. "And that's where the fish like to hang out. So get it out there."

I gritted my teeth and threw another cast. Harder this time. I watched my lure sail out over the water, coming down just behind those rocks. I started reeling. And then—wham!

"Oh!" I squealed.

"Lift the rod tip," Charlie instructed. "And keep reeling."

"Oh!" I cried louder. I could feel the fish fighting.

"Keep it steady," Charlie yelled. He waded into the water, net in hand. I continued bringing the line in and then Charlie bent and scooped my fish—my first fish!

I scrambled down the bank and rocks to get a closer look.

"It's a rainbow trout," Charlie said. "A nice one."

I gazed at the fish, admiring its silver scales and flashes of color. It was actually quite pretty, a beautiful piece of nature that I wanted to sketch and maybe write about later. "Is it okay?" I asked, worried.

"Yup. It's fine. Let's take a picture and then you can release it."

Charlie pulled the hook from my fish's mouth because I didn't want to do that part, and then I snapped a selfie of us posing with my fish. When we got done with that, Charlie showed me how to hold the fish so that I could place it back into the water.

I knelt and stuck my hands into Clover Creek. A second later my fish kicked and swam away. I straightened and looked at Charlie. "Yay!" I cheered, hugging him. "That was incredible!"

He smiled big. "You're a real fisherwoman now."

That first fish of mine . . . was also my last.

3

KNOW-NOTHING DIANA

I won't keep you in suspense. Charlie died. He died right in front of me.

The accident happened during our spring vacation, the same day that Charlie helped me catch my first fish, and even though I hadn't uttered a word since, my parents had me returning to sixth grade a couple of weeks later, hoping that might help. It didn't.

I entered the building and was immediately surrounded by stares and whispers. I kept my head down and pressed forward, but by the time I reached my locker I was struggling to breathe, and when I heard the hushed voices behind me, "There she is," and, "Poor Charlie," that was when everything went black.

Mom had to come and get me. Clearly, I wasn't ready for school. After that Mom moved her nursing shift to evenings so that she and I could homeschool during the day while Dad was teaching. My parents didn't make me go back to sixth grade for the remainder of the year, but they did sign me up with Know-Nothing Diana—a wretched grief counselor. Apparently, talking about a traumatic experience is part of the healing process, but I still hadn't said a word and I was most definitely not ready to talk about it with a stranger. Sadly, Know-Nothing Diana couldn't get that through her thick skull.

I would sit in her office—mute—and she would plow ahead asking me the same questions that I never answered at every one of our sessions. I couldn't tell if she was stubborn or stupid—or both. I decided on the latter when I heard her giving my parents her list of do's and don'ts, while also assuring them we were making progress. There was no telling how long this would've continued had that dingbat never crossed the line.

"You know, Thea, if you don't start talking soon, people will start filling in the silence for you, saying things like you pushed Charlie or that you tripped him," she warned. "Did you? Is that why you won't talk?"

How could she? I bolted from her office and didn't stop until I was in the parking lot. I had to get away. I needed air.

I don't know what that evil witch tried telling my parents after that, but that was the end of my sessions with Know-Nothing Diana. Mom and Dad had seen enough. It was time they took matters into their own hands. Together, they decided we needed a change—we were moving.

4

RUNNING AWAY

"How did we collect so much junk?" Dad complained in the midst of all the packing.

"That's what happens when you own a house," Mom replied. "Especially one with kids."

"Well, I'm not bringing it with us. We're getting rid of it," Dad declared.

His orders were simple: Sort through our stuff and throw out what we didn't need or want anymore. That was a good idea, except my little sisters didn't want to part with anything.

"No!" Abby cried when Dad tried trashing some of her ragged stuffies.

"No!" Livvy shrieked when Mom suggested donating a few of her old baby dolls.

What could you expect from seven- and eight-year-olds? They didn't get rid of anything—but who was I to talk? I didn't do any better.

Here was my problem: My junk equaled memories.

Like Charlie's spare EpiPen that I always carried in my backpack because he was highly allergic to bee stings. Or Roscoe, the stuffed bunny I got out of the prize box in first grade because I had the closest guess for how many jelly-beans were in Mrs. Hobby's jar. (Charlie saw where Mrs. Hobby had written down the answer and told me so that I could win. We were partners in crime from the beginning.) Then there was the Christmas card Charlie had given me. He drew a picture of Santa Claus dressed in swim trunks and sporting a snorkel mask and flippers because he was scared of the fat man wearing a red suit and large black boots. Even my nature drawings that had once decorated my walls reminded me of Charlie and our many trips to Clover Creek, which was why I'd taken them down and shoved them inside my desk after the accident.

Charlie had been gone for three months now, but I couldn't throw any of those things away. There were kids I was friendly with in school, but I'd never been good at making real friends, so when the only one you have dies . . . you're left with nothing. Those things, my junk, was all I had. But I also couldn't bring myself to look at it for too long. So I zipped my backpack closed, then put the bunny and card and the rest of my Charlie items into a small box and taped it shut—not knowing if I'd ever open it again.

Mom and Dad liked to say we were getting a fresh start, but the truth was we were running away. Hoping to get as far from the terrible past as possible. But I already knew, no matter how far we ran, I wasn't getting away from it—not ever.

5

SAYING GOODBYE

Packing the house was tedious and hard; saying good-bye to Charlie's parents was quick—but hardest of all. His parents were quite a bit older, but I loved them. They were like an extra set of grandparents, and I saw them all the time—until I didn't.

My sisters stayed in the car while Mom and Dad came to the door with me when we got there. Dad had phoned Charlie's parents to tell them we'd be coming so they were expecting us. This was my first time seeing Mrs. Gabriel since the day of the funeral, and I hadn't seen Mr. Gabriel since the accident. Mom and Dad had visited and gone to the services, but I skipped everything. I couldn't see Charlie dead—not again. I just couldn't. It wasn't until two weeks after they buried him that I finally had the courage to go see his grave.

His parents understood. Mrs. Gabriel had come to check on me after laying her son to rest. She walked into my bedroom and sat beside me. She took my hand and held it. "Thea, it's important you hear me say this," she said. "We don't blame you. This was a terrible accident. It makes no sense and I'm not sure it ever will, but it wasn't your fault."

That was nice of her, but she hadn't been there. Her words didn't make me feel less guilty.

By the time I reached the front step, his parents were already teary-eyed. So was I. Dad shook hands with Mr. Gabriel, while Mrs. Gabriel jumped straight to hugging me. Her wiry arms squeezed me tight and I felt every ounce of her love and pain.

"We've missed you," she said, holding me.

I was used to her always smelling like flour because she loved baking. She was constantly packing cookies and muffins and bread for Charlie and me to take with us on our excursions. She didn't smell like that today—and it made me sad.

"You be good and take care of yourself," she said, leaning back and looking at me. "Go and live life, Thea, and know you're always welcome to come back this way. We hope you do one day."

My jaw trembled. I nodded, even though I didn't know if that would ever happen. I handed her the small gift that I'd brought and had been holding the entire time; it was the one thing I hadn't dumped into the box with the rest of my Charlie things—a framed photo of Charlie and me after we'd returned from a day at Clover Creek, pieces of straw dangling from our mouths.

Mr. and Mrs. Gabriel both hugged me, and then I

turned and hurried back to the van while Mom and Dad finished saying their goodbyes. My little sisters didn't say a word when I climbed inside. Even they understood how hard that was. Mom and Dad joined us a few minutes later, and off we drove—running away.

6

NIGHTMARES

I'm alone, standing on the side of the road when the blacktop cracks and pulls apart. Charlie climbs out of the ground. He's dressed in his favorite khaki fishing vest— the same one he wore on our last day together. He's free of bruises and cuts and scrapes. He stares at me and I can see that he is sad and confused. Not even his lazy eye can hide that.

"Did you push me?" he asks, and it feels like a knife just plunged into my heart.

My face contorts. How could he? I open my mouth but no words come out. I'm unable to speak.

I reach to take his hand, but before I can touch him a fog descends and then a black SUV rounds the bend and is suddenly upon us. Its lights blind me. A cold wind blows across my skin as it races by—and then Charlie is gone.

* * *

I woke, shivering inside my new bedroom, real tears wetting my cheeks. I sat up and hugged my pillow tight. Just as I feared, we'd moved clear across the state, but my nightmares followed me. I was unpacked, but I wasn't settled. I was alone—and missing my best friend.

7

DAD LOSES HIS MIND

Dad was driving Cleopatra, our ancient green minivan. Mom was riding shotgun, my sisters were in the way back, and I sat in one of the middle seats. We were on our way home from the grocery store. When you move into a new house you've got a refrigerator and cabinets to restock.

I was old enough to stay home alone and even watch my sisters, but Know-Nothing Diana had told my parents she didn't think me being alone was a good idea just yet. Whatever. Mom and Dad agreed that dimwit didn't know anything, but they still chose to adhere to that piece of her advice. So anyway, thanks to my long-gone wretched grief counselor, I was present when my sisters started fighting.

"Don't touch me," Abby said.

"Don't touch me," Livvy mimicked.

"Don't look at me," Abby said.

"Don't look at me," Livvy repeated.

"Puke face."

"Butt face."

"MOM!" they yelled.

"GIRLS!" Mom roared. "That's enough! Nobody wants to hear it."

Actually, it wasn't bothering me. Their fighting was one of the few things that hadn't changed. But I don't want to mislead you and make you think my sisters were always fighting, because they weren't—not always. As Dad liked to say, Liv and Abby managed to get along twenty-three out of the twenty-four hours in a day, but during that one hour when they decided to go at it, he wanted to run and hide. Their knock-down-drag-outs always happened during that stretch of time when they ran out of things to do and got bored or tired.

Well, there certainly wasn't much for them to do way in the back of Cleopatra and we were all more than a little tired after the big move, so let the fireworks begin. As soon as Mom scolded them their crying commenced—and that was worse than the arguing. Poor Dad had nowhere to run and hide. What happened next changed everything.

"Let's get a puppy," he blurted.

All fighting and crying stopped immediately.

"What?" Mom asked.

"A puppy," Dad said.

"Yay!" my sisters screamed.

"What?!" Mom cried. "Have you lost your mind?"

We hadn't had a dog since Sparky, which was almost

four years ago, so it was safe to say Dad's sudden announcement took us by surprise. If it weren't for Mom's shock, I would've guessed this was another one of Know-Nothing Diana's brilliant stupid suggestions, but it was actually Dad's dumb idea all on his own.

"Do you want to get a puppy?" Dad repeated.

"Yeah!" Livvy and Abby screamed in return.

I continued staring out the window. What I wanted was to have my best friend back, but that was impossible. That wasn't anything a dog could fix, so I didn't care.

"Andy, what're you doing?" Mom said, all sorts of concern in her voice. "You know you can't mention a puppy and then go back on it. You can't do that to the girls."

"I know," Dad said.

Livvy and Abby were wild with excitement. Their celebration reached new heights. They broke into a crazy cheer, singing loudly.

"We're getting a puu-py! We're getting a puu-py! We're getting a puu-py!"

"Not if you don't stop the fighting," Mom threatened.

"Yeah," Dad agreed. "And by the way, everybody says the two of you look like me so I don't appreciate those Puke-face and Butt-face comments."

I cracked a rare smile. Dad was on a roll. But his dog idea was still a stupid one.

8

RESEARCH

Dad claimed it was the perfect time for us to get a dog, but I didn't know who he thought he was fooling. It would've been much smarter to get one before moving. Then the puppy could've had all of its potty accidents in our old house rather than our new one. Not to mention that would've given my sisters the summer to devote to training their puppy—not mine!—but there was no turning back now.

Mom got her computer out as soon as we got home. She huddled with my sisters on the couch and began surfing the web in hopes of finding our future dog. I helped Dad with the groceries and then I went and sat in our recliner. (I would've gone to my room, but Mom wouldn't go for that. Even if I wasn't talking, she wanted me with them and not alone.)

"For starters, we need to decide what kind of dog we want," Mom said. "Labs make great family dogs."

"Sparky was a Lab," Livvy said.

"I don't remember Sparky," Abby whined.

"You probably wouldn't," Mom replied. "You had only just turned three when he—"

Mom stopped short before finishing her sentence. I could feel her cringing. According to Know-Nothing Diana, "died" was the type of word to avoid using around me because it could trigger an emotional breakdown. And the general topic of death was a big no-no. Whatever. Told you that woman was an idiot. Like I needed any stupid word to remind me of what had happened to Charlie. It wasn't like I ever forgot.

"I want a little dog," Abby cried.

"One that we can dress up," Livvy agreed.

"I'm not getting a purse dog so you two can dress it up!" Dad yelled. He stuck his head into the living room. "That's where I draw the line. You can do that with your dolls. I need a boy dog. I live with all women now."

Liv and Abby stuck their tongues out at him.

"Go away," Mom said. "We'll call you when we have one we like."

"Find a boy dog," Dad ordered before returning to the kitchen. I could smell that he was beginning to make dinner but I wasn't hungry.

Mom and my sisters turned back to the computer and read all about Labs, golden retrievers, terriers, Chihuahuas, and even Saint Bernards. Mom read aloud so it was easier for my sisters, but I knew she was also trying to include me. Not happening. Still not interested.

My sisters thought every dog sounded fun, so after a while Mom changed gears and started looking to see what dogs were actually available and nearby. That was when she discovered rescue shelters.

"What's a rescue shelter?" Abby asked.

"Well, in some areas there are places that . . ."

"That what?" Abby said. She didn't understand why Mom had stopped midsentence.

I could feel Mom cringing—again. "Killed" definitely had to be on Know-Nothing Diana's list of words and topics to avoid.

"That what?!" Abby screeched.

"That kill dogs!" Livvy exclaimed. She was reading off the website.

"Why do they kill the doggies?" Abby asked, confused and upset.

"Well, sweetie. A dogcatcher finds doggies that are without owners and turns them over to a shelter where they are housed, but if the doggie is sick or if no one claims them or adopts them, then they might be euthanized. They don't have enough space to keep all of them."

"What's your-in-hized?" Abby asked.

"You-then-ized," Livvy said. "It means put to sleep forever."

"That's sad."

"Yes, and a lot of people agree with you," Mom said. "So that's why there are groups who rescue dogs from these shelters and then transport them to new places where they try to keep them until they do find families. These groups and places make up rescue shelters."

"Let's get one from there," Abby said. "I want to save a doggie!"

"Me, too!" Livvy agreed, which didn't happen often.

So Mom started researching rescue shelters and found one that was only an hour away. Hickory Rescue Shelter had pictures of dogs on their website that had recently been adopted and pictures of current residents.

"Look at that little puppy," Abby squealed.

"He looks just like Sparky," Mom said.

"It's so cute," Livvy said. "Let's get it."

"Can we, pleeease?" my sisters begged.

"Oh," Mom replied, her voice much lower now. "She's a girl."

"Can we get her, pleeease?" my sisters pleaded.

"Shhh," Mom whispered. "We'll go first thing tomorrow morning, but don't tell your father who we found. Once he sees her, he'll have to say yes. He's got a soft spot in his heart for girls."

My sisters giggled about their special secret.

"Thea, come see the puppy we found," Abby whispered.

I shook my head.

"Tomorrow," Mom said. "Thea will get to see her tomorrow."

I turned away and stared out the window. I didn't care about any dog.

9

———

A NEW NIGHTMARE

Nightmares continued to haunt me, and that was no different on the eve of getting our puppy. But the nightmare that came for me that night was different.

We're walking, me and my dog, down the side of the road. My dog is wet because he's been swimming. He's happy. His tail wags and his ears stand tall. I'm happy.

But then the sky goes dark. The warm sun disappears and an eerie wind picks up. I feel it blow across my skin and I shiver. A low moan vibrates in the distance. And then it is there. The black SUV rounds the bend and is upon us. There is no time to react. I feel the leash get ripped from my hand.

My dog is gone.

I woke up drenched in sweat, feeling exhausted. My heart raced and my muscles felt like I'd been flexing and squeezing them for hours. None of that was different from my other nightmares—but that dog was.

I left my bed and walked downstairs to the living room and climbed into the recliner. I sat there hugging my knees to my chest.

I loved that dog in my dream—but I didn't want him.

10

THE CRATE IS MOST IMPORTANT

We drove for an hour: Dad behind the wheel, Mom riding shotgun, my sisters in the way back—not fighting—and me in the middle seat, not saying anything. I couldn't have snuck in a word even if I'd wanted to, not with the way everyone else was going on and on about the puppy we were going to get.

"You'll need to keep track of your stuff," Mom warned us for the hundredth time. "Puppies like to chew things."

Whatever.

"And there will be no feeding him from the table. And he stays off the furniture," Dad reminded us for the millionth time.

Tell my sisters. It's their dog, not mine.

"And she's going to sleep with me?" Livvy said.

"No fair! I want her to sleep with me," Abby whined.

"I called it first," Livvy argued.

"Stop saying 'she,'" Dad said. "We're getting a boy, and he's not sleeping with either of you. He sleeps in his crate until he can go without making accidents in the house. The crate is the most important part in training a puppy. It's where he'll feel safe and want to spend time."

"And when she's done with the crate she can take turns sleeping with us," Abby said.

"He," Dad emphasized.

"We'll see," Mom said.

Mom and Dad talked like they were dog whisperers, but as we'd soon find out, they were no match for our future puppy. We didn't end up with your average dog—not by a long shot.

11

HICKORY RESCUE SHELTER

We pulled into Hickory Rescue Shelter and my sisters jumped out of Cleopatra before Dad even had her in park. A chorus of barks and yaps and deep-longing howls immediately welcomed us.

"Ohh!" my sisters squealed. "Can we go see them?"

"We need to stop by the office first to let them know we're here," Mom said.

"Hurry up," Abby yelled, running ahead with Livvy. "We want to see the doggies."

I was happy to lengthen my stride. Anything to escape all those sad songs. The dogs' cries sounded like my heart felt.

"May I help you?" the woman at the counter asked once the five of us were inside.

"Yes," Mom answered. "We'd like to get a puppy."

"Well, you're in the right place then," the woman said. She smiled at Liv and Abby. "My name is Rebecca. You can follow me outside and we'll see if we have one you like."

"We already know which one we want," Abby blurted. "We saw her on your computer."

Liv tried to cover Abby's mouth, but she was too late. The cat was out of the bag. To be honest, I was surprised she'd kept their secret this long. Secret-keeping wasn't exactly Abby's strength.

Dad scowled. He cast Mom and my sisters a dirty look, but it wasn't a for-real one. The truth was he was going to do whatever made them happy, even if that meant a female dog. Mom was right about Dad having a soft spot in his heart for girls. My sisters had him wrapped around their little fingers. Unfortunately, there wasn't anything Dad could do for me. I wished it was that easy, but it wasn't.

"And which dog would that be?" Rebecca asked.

"We saw a nine-week-old female black Lab mix," Mom said.

"Oh, you mean Chloe . . . ? I'm afraid she's already gone," Rebecca said. "She was a cutie, so she wasn't here very long. I'm sorry."

"Aw," Liv and Abby groaned, their bodies sagging.

"Don't worry," Rebecca said. "We still have plenty of other wonderful puppies waiting for you."

We followed her out to the shelter, where the dogs were still barking and howling their heads off, but the moment Rebecca opened the door, they stopped. We stepped inside behind her.

"Take your time and let me know if you find one you like," she said. "If you do, I can let you take the pup into the play yard we have out back. That way you have a chance to try the dog on for size."

"You mean we get to try out the puppies like trying on shoes?" Livvy asked.

"Something like that," Rebecca said, and chuckled.

"Daddy takes forever buying shoes," Abby said.

"Well, unlike shoes, these pups will help you make the decision," Rebecca said. "You'll see."

Did she mean to suggest the dog would pick us? Because I wasn't buying that. The only person who'd ever picked me for anything was Charlie.

It happened way back in the beginning of first grade, when we were getting ready to study the life cycle of frogs. Mrs. Hobby was very excited because for the first time she was able to get live specimens. We were really lucky. She explained that we'd be working with our partners over the next several weeks to draw sketches and record notes and observations like real scientists.

Charlie picked me as soon as she was done talking. "You wanna be my partner? All the boys make fun of me because of my eye, and you have dirt under your fingernails, so I know you're not gonna be all girly about the frogs."

"What's wrong with your eye?" I asked him. I'd been curious since day one but never said anything.

"I can't open it all the way or get it to go straight. The doctor calls it a lazy eye, but I think that's dumb because it works hard."

I giggled. Charlie was funny. I liked him from the beginning.

12

DOG SHOPPING

It was like walking down an aisle in the grocery store, except instead of finding chips and crackers on one side and mac-n-cheese on the other, there were puppies on display. My sisters couldn't contain their excitement.

"Oh my gosh!" Abby squealed. "Look at this one!"

"Look at this one!" Livvy echoed.

It was puppy overload. Up and down the aisle, back and forth, my sisters took turns squealing.

I kept my head down and slowly moved forward. I didn't want to look at the dogs, but I could feel them staring. Staring at me just like all those eyes did in school when I tried to go back after the accident. I couldn't take it.

I spun around and hurried out the door. I needed air. I found a lonely picnic table on the side of the building and sat there while I waited for my sisters to make up their minds.

I'd wanted a dog for so long. I'd wanted to make all

those special memories like Mom and Dad had with Sparky. But not now. Not anymore. My nightmare was a warning. I couldn't keep my dog safe, couldn't stop bad things from happening to him.

Charlie and I were walking along side by side, on our way back home from a day of fishing and exploring Clover Creek, when a doe and her fawn came out of the woods and started to cross the road just ahead of us.

I gasped. "Charlie, look!" I urged, trying to keep my voice low. But the deer heard me and froze. Mama and baby stood in middle of the road, staring at us through the thickening fog.

The black SUV that came around the bend had nowhere to go. It swerved to miss the deer.

It should've been me walking next to the road, not Charlie. Charlie was the better person. The last project we did in fifth grade had us write about what we wanted to be when we grew up. I talked all about working for *National Geographic,* studying and drawing nature and writing scientific articles. Everybody picked specific careers and jobs like me—everybody except Charlie. He wrote that he wanted to do something special. Something he'd be remembered for. He never got the chance.

"Thea, we're going in the play yard," Livvy yelled, waking me from my daydreams.

"C'mon!" Abby squealed, bouncing up and down. "C'mon! We're going in the play yard with a puppy. We've got to see if it's the right one."

I shook my head.

Abby's bouncing stopped. She was disappointed, but I just couldn't get myself to do it. "Will you always be sad?" she asked.

I tightened my jaw, fighting the knot that had grabbed the inside of my throat.

"I hope not," Abby said. She gave me a hug and then she took Livvy's hand and the two of them turned around and went back inside—without their sad big sister.

13

THE PUPPY
IN SPACE NUMBER NINE

Dad came out next. He walked over and sat next to me. I wiped my eyes.

"Hey, honey." He waited but I didn't say anything. "I have to ask you to join us now. Rebecca needs the whole family to go into the play yard so she can make sure the puppy is comfortable with all of us. It's their policy."

I didn't move. I sat in a daze, staring at the different stones scattered around the picnic table.

"You can stand off to the side," Dad said. "You don't have to interact with the puppy if you don't want to, but I need you to do this—for your sisters."

I slid off the table and Dad wrapped his arm around my shoulders. "Thank you," he whispered.

I walked beside him, my gaze on the ground and then the floor when we reentered the kennel and started down the puppy aisle. The play yard was out the door on the other end of the building.

"Wait till you see this pup," Dad said. "The only bad thing is it's a girl."

I give Dad credit for trying, but I still didn't care. I wasn't even going to look at the dog my sisters had picked. But then something happened that made me look. Not at the puppy waiting outside, but at the one in space number nine. The puppy in number nine stuck his paw through the chain-link gate and reached out as far as he could and touched me on the shin when I came by.

I stopped. He pulled his paw back and sat there, waiting for me. My breath caught when I saw his lazy eye. That little white puppy with a brindle mask and one big brindle spot on his side was the cutest thing in the whole world—and he had picked me.

I bent down to the pup's level, gripping the fence between us. "Don't worry," I whispered, so that only he could hear me. "You can still be amazing with that lazy eye. My friend, Charlie, was."

That was the first time I'd spoken, the first time I'd said Charlie's name out loud since he died—even if it was only a tiny whisper. The puppy licked my fingers and in a few seconds he had them all wet, same as my eyes. I glanced up at Dad.

"We can take him into the play yard next," he said, reading my mind. "That one is a boy," he added, squeezing my shoulder.

I turned back to the puppy and smiled. His tail wagged.

14

IN THE PLAY YARD

"Huh!" Mom gasped when she first saw the dog. "Are you sure this is a good idea, Andy? I mean—"

"The dog picked her," Dad explained. "You should've seen it. He just reached out and touched her."

"But can he run and play like a normal puppy?" Abby asked. She too had noticed his eye and she was worried that it would slow him down.

In response, the dog ducked under Abby's reach and dashed around behind her. He nosed her butt and then he did the same to Livvy. Mom let out a high-pitched squeal when he goosed her next.

"Don't even think about it," Dad warned, pointing at the little rascal. "I'm the alpha around here."

The dog trotted over and licked Dad's outstretched finger.

Mom snorted. "Even he knows that's a joke."

"Did you find one you like?" Rebecca asked, joining us in the play yard.

"We want this one!" Liv and Abby cheered. "Can we get him?"

Mom and Dad exchanged glances and nodded.

My sisters ran up and hugged me. "Thank you, Thea!"

My heart swelled. And it swelled even more when our new pup squeezed his way in between us so that he wasn't left out.

"Told you it was time," Dad bragged to Mom.

15

A NAME AND A COLLAR

"What're you going to name your new puppy?" Rebecca asked when we were back inside the office.

"Clifford!" Abby cheered.

"No!" Liv objected. "He's white, not red. Let's name him Snoopy."

"No!" Abby whined. "His name is Clifford."

"Snoopy!" Liv argued.

"Clifford!" Abby persisted.

"Girls!" Mom yelled. "That's enough."

"Tell you what," Rebecca interrupted. "I'm going to write down Jack as a temporary name, and after you've spent more time with your pup, you can decide on a real name to give him. Okay?"

"I kinda like Jack for his permanent name," Dad said.

"Me too," Mom agreed.

"We can call him Jack-Jack if we want," Abby said.

"Or JJ for short," Livvy said.

"Or Jackson," Dad added. "For when he's in trouble."

Dad locked eyes with our new puppy, trying to act all serious and show him he meant business, but he cracked a smile almost immediately. Dad had a soft spot in his heart for his girls and his dog.

"Well, let me just say I'm really happy you girls have picked Mr. Jack," Rebecca said. "He deserves a special family. He hasn't had the easiest start in life."

"What do you mean?" Livvy asked.

"Jack was abandoned at a very young age," Rebecca said.

"What's abandit?" Abby asked next.

"It means he was left all alone with no one to take care of him," Dad answered.

"As a baby?" Abby whined.

Rebecca nodded. "Most likely. And probably because of his lazy eye. But luckily, someone with a good heart stumbled upon Jack before it was too late. The nice man got him to a local vet, and from there he eventually made his way here, to Hickory Rescue Shelter. He arrived scrawny and needed lots of care, but Jack's a fighter. I think the hardest part has been watching every family pass him by—always because of his eye."

"Not us," Livvy declared.

"That's right. Not you," Rebecca replied.

"That's right," Abby agreed.

Rebecca smiled. "Maybe you girls can pick out a collar for Mr. Jack while I finish up the paperwork with your mom and dad," she suggested.

"Okay!" Liv and Abby cheered.

I followed my sisters to the back of the office, where they had various dog supplies for sale. I brought Jack with me so he could try the collar on. Livvy pulled a blue one off the rack and Abby chose a green one. This had the makings of another fight written all over it, but Jack saved us from that when he walked over and grabbed the red collar in his mouth.

"He likes the red one with the fishies on it," Abby said.

"Put it on him, Thea," Liv said.

Seeing the trout design gave me a funny feeling in my stomach, but I wrapped the collar around Jack's neck and snapped the ends together. A perfect fit.

"All right, girls. Time to take Jack home," Dad said.

PART II

16

BONDING OVER TRAINING

Jack's lazy eye reminded me of Charlie, but so did his boundless energy and love for the outdoors. I didn't recognize it right away because Jack was a little shy when we first got him home, not to mention exhausted from the day's events, but come the next morning he was ready to show his true colors.

Liv and Abby had picked out several toys to go along with Jack's collar before leaving the shelter yesterday, but the thing Jack chose to play with—when no one was looking—was Dad's shoe. It only took five minutes of us not paying attention and Jack-Jack had half the sole chewed and several teeth marks poked through the top. Not a smart move for a dog who would need to convince the same guy to bypass the crate, but I'm getting ahead of myself. The crate saga comes next.

"Take that dog outside now!" Dad bellowed when he found Jack chomping his loafer. "He needs to burn off some energy!"

My sisters were upstairs doing who-knows-what, so Dad's order fell to me. I grabbed a handful of treats and Jack-Jack's leash and out the door we hurried—before Dad blew his top. Truth be told, I didn't mind. I'd done some research of my own on training your dog and teaching basic commands before going to bed last night, and I wanted to give it a try.

First things first, though. Before beginning your training session, you need to play with your dog to get the craziness out, otherwise you'll never get your pet to listen and be attentive.

I found a stick on the ground and threw it across the yard. Jack-Jack barreled after it and then automatically brought it back to me so that I could throw it again. Over and over we played fetch. Jack-Jack loved our new game. The only time he stopped was when he had to go potty. (I left that so my sisters could learn how to clean up after their dog.)

After a good amount of fetching, I decided to attempt lesson number one. I started with the basic *sit* command. The videos I'd watched claimed if I held the treat in my hand and moved it from the front of Jack's head back over the top, he would sit in response. I didn't even need to say anything. It worked! We did that one a bunch of times.

Next, I moved on to *stay*. Again, using the simple hand gestures I'd seen in the videos worked. Each time Jack did it right, I gave him a treat and rubbed his side and scratched him behind the ears. When he looked at me, his tail wagging and tongue dangling out the side of his mouth, that was the closest I'd come to feeling anything near happy in a long time.

I introduced my command for *come* last because that was supposed to be the hardest order to teach. I decided to use a specific whistle because I wasn't about to yell, and a whistle seemed like something a dog could hear from a great distance.

First I attached Jack to his leash, because it was needed for this lesson. Then I let him wander around, and when he got far enough away from me, I whistled and pulled him back to my side so he could start to associate those two things with each other.

Jack-Jack was a quick learner. I had him coming on my whistle without pulling his leash in just a few minutes. Of course, this was with no distractions—add a squirrel or another dog to the mix and I could probably forget about getting him to listen, but this was a start.

At this point, I figured we'd done enough training for one day and Dad had had enough time to cool off, so I started back toward the house, but Jack-Jack had other ideas. He wasn't ready yet. It seemed he wanted to spend more time outside.

I hadn't gone for a walk since the accident. Being out on streets made me jumpy. But Jack-Jack tugged at the leash, wanting to go. Those puppy eyes, the lazy one included, did me in. It was almost like Jack knew I could do it.

Our leash walk was important for two major reasons:

(1) I learned that Jack was terrified of any and all loud noises, especially roaring engines. He cowered and shrank as far away from the road as possible every time a large truck came by. I wondered what had happened that gave him such fear. And (2) it proved to me that I could go for a walk and I'd be okay; Jack was right—and this was important for what was coming.

17

MOM'S NON-NEGOTIABLES

In total, we got to spend three days at home with our new puppy, but then it was time for Jack to go into his crate for real, not for the night when sleeping by Dad's bedside, and not for the short practice sessions Dad had been doing with him over the weekend. But All. Day. Long. Why? Because school was starting, and Mom had two non-negotiables: (1) I absolutely had to return to school, and (2) we absolutely had to get back to sitting together as a family for dinner each night, which was something that we'd stopped doing after the accident. Family dinner was our chance to talk about our days—*fun* (with an eye roll).

I listened when we gathered at the table that first night, but I didn't contribute. Jack-Jack was still the only one I'd managed to talk to and he settled next to my chair, happy to listen along with me. Besides, I didn't have anything to say. Seventh grade was fine, which I considered a success. Being the new kid was scary, but I handled all the stares and whispers associated with that much better than I had all the stares and whispers that were about Charlie. I passed through the day without talking to anyone and no one tried talking to me. Middle school was easy like that. It was much bigger than elementary school, and we switched rooms and teachers and class-mates for every subject, so I didn't need to worry about any of that getting-to-know-each-other garbage. Science was the highlight, not because we actually got to do much, but because it had always been my favorite part of school. The only tricky time was lunch, but I just snuck into the bathroom and hid there. Lunch didn't last that long, so it wasn't as bad as it sounds.

Liv and Abby, on the other hand, had an interesting situation. They were in a combined second-and-third-grade classroom, which meant they were stuck together even during school. That could spell disaster, but it didn't seem to bother them. They couldn't wait to tell us about their first days. They loved their new teacher, Ms. Stacy. She was pretty and smart and the best reader because she made great voices and on and on and on. The two of them would've talked all night long, but Dad finally cut them off. Why? Because we had to talk about Jack. Turned out he had the most exciting day.

18

THE NOT-SO-PERFECT CRATE

After my successful weekend of leash walking with Jack, Mom and Dad decided it was my responsibility to meet my sisters after school to walk home with them. It was either that or they had to make the trip alone because neither Mom nor Dad could leave their new jobs in time to pick them up. Had the trek involved back roads, I never would've been able to do it, but the path from school was a straight shot down Salem Street, where there were sidewalks the entire way, and Jack had already shown me I could do it.

I stood on the corner across from Johnny Arena Elementary waiting for my sisters when they got dismissed on their first day. At that time of afternoon, we had the sun shining bright on our backs, creating long shadows that stretched in front of us. Liv and Abby kept busy playing shadow tag and shadow poses, while I kept my eyes peeled for any sudden black SUVs. But it wasn't anything I saw that scared me, it was what I heard. We weren't even in the driveway yet when the sounds of Jack's manic barking reached us.

"Jack-Jack!" Abby cried.

We took off running.

The moment we opened the door to the house Jack stopped. We rushed into the kitchen where Dad had positioned the crate and found our puppy soaking wet, but not in pee, as you might be thinking. The bottom of Jack's crate was covered in a layer of slobber about an inch thick. It was disgusting, not to mention the spit splattered up and down every nearby wall and all over the surrounding floor. Jack's eyes were completely bloodshot and his tongue dangled out the side of his mouth—but his tail wagged when he saw us.

"He's all wet and he smells," Abby whined.

"Let him out!" Livvy implored.

Together, my sisters and I got things cleaned up and Jack-Jack toweled off. When we finished drying him, he walked over and downed an entire bowl of water. Then he found his bed and crashed, utterly exhausted.

The only thing we hadn't bought brand-new for Jack was his crate. According to Dad, he still had the biggest, baddest, strongest one ever made left over from Sparky. That crate had worked perfectly for Spark, so there was no reason not to use it for Jack.

"You don't mess with a good thing," Dad said, "especially when it comes to the crate. The crate is—"

"The most important part in training a puppy," Livvy finished. "We know."

"Blah, blah, blah," Abby added.

Mom laughed. My sisters were right. We'd heard Dad say this about a hundred times.

"Well, it is," Dad stressed. "Jack's going to love it. You'll see."

We saw all right. Jack *hated* his crate, which explains why he became the main topic of conversation at dinner that night.

"Ms. Stacy sounds lovely," Dad said, interrupting my sisters, "but we need to talk about Jackson."

At the sound of his name Jack picked his head up and looked at me.

"Do you think he was barking all day?" Dad asked.

"There was a layer of slobber on the bottom of his crate!" Livvy emphasized.

"And on the floor and the walls too," Abby added.

Mom sighed. "This letter sure makes it sound like he was."

The letter she was referring to came from an anonymous neighbor who, at the time of writing, wanted us to know that our dog's incessant barking had been going on for more than an hour. The letter writer hoped we could do something to prevent that from continuing beyond the next few days—nice of them to give us a little time—or else they were prepared to take more drastic measures, such as calling animal control and the police.

I reached down and gave Jack a reassuring pet. I didn't care about any letter. I wasn't going to let anything bad happen to him. It would all work out—I hoped.

Round and round Mom and Dad went about what to do, but the truth was they didn't have a clue. They never expected Jack to have an issue with his crate.

"Maybe he'll be okay tomorrow, now that he knows we'll be home and we're not leaving him for good," Dad said.

"Really, you think it's that simple?" Mom asked, sounding doubtful. I was thinking the same thing.

"I'll leave his towel with him. That should give him some comfort, like a little kid's blankie does. You'll see."

Dad's famous last words.

19

ON REPEAT

The first two weeks of school were on repeat. I slid through each day unnoticed—not talking to anyone and not having anything to say at dinner. I liked it that way and so did my sisters because they always had lots to share. Jack-Jack liked it too. He had his favorite spot beside my chair, where he lay for story time every night.

First, it was Liv and Abby's class pet that they couldn't stop talking about. The "pet" was nothing more than a glorified stuffed bunny named Snowball that the kids took turns taking home. The bunny came with a journal that the children had to write in, telling about Snowball's adventures with their family. Pretty lame, but Liv and Abby thought it was amazing.

Better yet was their classroom mystery box. Each week a different student got to take the mystery box home to choose an object to hide in it. When returned, the kids would line up, and one after the other they'd reach inside the box to feel the hidden object and try to guess what it was. If you guessed correctly you got to pick something out of Ms. Stacy's prize bin, but if no one guessed correctly then the hider got the prize—and according to Liv and Abby, Ms. Stacy had the best prizes! They loved the mystery box, but they hated that Simon always pushed his way to the front of the line and got to go first.

Actually, Simon was the only thing my sisters didn't seem to like about school. I'd heard that boy's name more than any other. The kid wouldn't leave them alone. According to their stories, he was always touching Abby's papers and taking her pencils, bothering her when she was trying to do her work, and he pestered Livvy on the playground. But all my sisters got from Mom was your classic unhelpful-adult advice.

"Oh, girls. I'm sure that little boy likes you. That's why he won't leave you alone."

That was all they got because Mom and Dad had bigger fish to fry than some twerp named Simon. The crate situation had not improved. Dad had relocated Jack to the main bathroom so our neighbors couldn't hear his barking, but beyond that, nothing Dad tried seemed to help.

Whenever we left Jack, he went nuts. And I mean crazy nuts. Dad had started recording him with an old video camera so that we could see just how bad it was. Jack was a lunatic. Grabbing the bars in his mouth, biting and squeezing them. Slamming and pawing and jumping against the gate. And barking. His barking never stopped.

If we left anything inside the crate, it was destroyed. Towel ripped to shreds. Ducky gutted and no longer quacking. Dad even tried some special vest that was supposed to fit Jack snugly and calm him down. Forget it. Nothing worked.

"I called the vet to ask her advice," Dad announced at dinner, sounding defeated. He and Mom were at their wits' end. I was beginning to worry they might say we had to give Jack up if we couldn't find a solution soon.

"And?" Mom asked.

"She suggested we try a frozen KONG filled with peanut butter."

"That's it? A KONG filled with frozen peanut butter is going to fix everything? Did you tell her how bad he is in the crate?"

"I told her we were struggling," Dad said, lowering his head.

"Struggling! Andy, the dog goes berserk. You've seen him. He needs drugs."

"The KONG is going to work," Dad said, trying to sound optimistic.

I glanced down at Jack and I swear even he raised his eyebrows at the suggestion.

"Fine," Mom said. "You try your amazing KONG trick, but when it doesn't work—"

"I'll call the vet back and ask her about starting an anxiety medicine."

"No. You'll *tell* her we want to start an anxiety medicine," Mom said, putting her foot down.

"Maybe we should try leaving him out of the crate," Livvy suggested.

Instantly, Jack's tail started wagging.

"Fat chance," Dad said. "Do you want him to destroy our house?"

"Maybe he won't," Abby said.

"Have you seen what he does to the things we leave in the crate? Out of the question," Dad said.

Jack's tail stopped.

If Dad had listened to my sisters, it would've saved him a lot of headaches. If Mom had listened to my sisters, maybe I wouldn't have had to take the Simon situation into my own hands.

20

REPEAT INTERRUPTED

Two weeks of school without incident, without being noticed—and then that all changed. The classroom intercom beeped in the middle of science class.

"Excuse me, Mr. Morris," interrupted a voice.

My teacher paused the video about volcanoes that we were watching. "Yes?" he replied.

"Would you please send Thea Ettinger down to the office?"

"Thea?" he repeated, clearly confused.

The man didn't even know I existed—and I liked it that way. But annoying-intercom lady had just blown my cover. And with my classmates too.

"The weird girl's name is Thea?" one of the dumb boys whispered.

"Guess so," his buddy responded.

"Hey, Thea. See ya. Wouldn't wanna be ya," the first boy sang, which got laughs from the rest of the class.

No, you wouldn't, I thought.

I didn't acknowledge the jerks and I didn't wait around for Mr. Morris to try anything stupid, like attempting to talk to me. I was a little bummed about missing the rest of the video but I grabbed my things and bolted.

I made my way to the office, wondering why I was even being called down. It wasn't like I'd done anything wrong. I thought about not showing up, but that seemed like a surefire way to end up on people's radars, so I sucked it up and went.

"Can I help you?" the woman behind the front desk asked when I entered. It was annoying-intercom lady. She even looked annoying.

I shrugged.

"Did you need something?"

Again, I shrugged.

"Well, I'm not a mind reader, so unless you start talking, I'm not—"

"Thea?" a different woman asked after entering the office behind me.

I turned around and nodded.

"Thank you, Rita," the new woman said to the annoying one. "I'll take it from here."

I followed the new woman out of the main office and into a smaller room around the corner.

"Have a seat," she said, gesturing to the sofa beside her desk.

I sat.

"I'm Ms. Riley, the seventh-grade guidance counselor. I had you called down because I like to meet with all of our new students, just to check in and make sure everything is going well. So . . . how is everything going?"

I nodded.

"Off to a good start. You're finding your way around okay?"

More nodding.

"No problems with classes?"

I shook my head.

"That's good." Ms. Riley shifted in her chair and flipped open a folder on her desk. "There was something else I wanted to mention. I was looking through your file and it says here that you recently endured a traumatic event. I just wanted you to know that I'm here for you if you'd like to talk about it."

Like to talk about it? Was this woman for real? Was I talking at all? How dumb was she? Seriously, who certified these people? I got up from my seat and walked out. I was ready for her to try stopping me, but to her credit, Ms. Riley was smart enough to let me go.

Science was still in session, but I was in no shape to go back there, so I hid in the bathroom until it was over, my mind racing. The question I wanted answered was why had Mom given my old school permission to put anything about the accident in my file? There wasn't anybody here that I'd ever want to talk to about Charlie. I was trying to move on from Charlie. I thought she knew that. The more I ruminated over it, the angrier I got. And I was ruminating all the way till dinner.

21

DINNER BLOW-UP

The peanut butter KONG didn't help. It kept Jack busy for a few minutes, but then he spent the rest of the day going beserko—like usual.

"I'll call the vet tomorrow," Dad promised, once everyone was seated at the table and Jack had taken his spot by my chair.

Mom didn't even acknowledge him. "How were your days?" she asked, turning to my sisters and me. She was beyond done with Dad and his stupid crate.

"I brought home the mystery box!" Abby exclaimed. "I get to hide something and if nobody guesses then I get to reach into Ms. Stacy's prize bin."

"Only if Simon doesn't ruin it," Livvy grumbled. "Last time he dumped the object out of the box so the rest of us didn't get a turn."

"That's great," Mom said.

That's great. That was what she said. That's great! Why? Because she wasn't listening! I was frustrated for my sisters. And angry. I wasn't even in their class and I was sick of this Simon kid. He was your classic behavioral issue that the teacher and school couldn't handle. That was all fine and good until you were the one stuck putting up with the jerk. The boy probably had a file an inch thick. *A file.* I couldn't hold it in any longer. I was on my feet.

"The stupid guidance counselor called me into her office today," I exploded, startling everyone at the table. After all, I didn't talk. "She wanted to know about—" I stopped, fighting the sudden lump in my throat. "About the traumatic event mentioned in my file," I croaked.

"What?" Mom exclaimed.

I glared at her.

"Thea, I didn't think anyone would try talking to you about it. I'm sorry."

I couldn't keep the tears from coming. I turned from the table and ran to my room.

22

LOYAL JACK-JACK

I collapsed onto my bed, sobbing and clinging to my pillow. It wasn't my parents who came after me, but Jack-Jack. He hopped up next to me and rooted and weaseled his way under my arms until he was snuggled between me and my pillow. He nosed my neck and licked my salty cheeks.

I pulled him close and squeezed him tight. "Jack-Jack, I don't want to forget Charlie, but remembering him still hurts," I whispered into his fur. "I wasn't ready for Ms. Riley to ask about his accident."

I sniffled and Jack licked my chin.

"You have Charlie's eyes, Jack-Jack. Every time I look at you, I see him." My voice caught.

Immediately, Jack gave me another round of kisses. I swear he was listening and doing his best to tell me it was going to be all right.

My loyal dog stayed by my side, never moving an inch. Eventually, I drifted off to sleep. The emotional roller coaster of the day had taken its toll and left me exhausted—but I did not find rest.

I'm standing on the bank of Clover Creek, watching Charlie cast and reel, in awe of his skill and the beauty of it. "Why do you like fishing so much?" I ask.

"It's not just fishing; it's nature," Charlie says. "Nature doesn't judge people. Doesn't care what we look like or how much money we have. I like that."

"You talk like some great philosopher. I'll have to start calling you Charlie Aristotle or Charlie Plato," I tease.

"I'm not any philosopher and I'm not even all that smart. I just see things different than most. It's because of my eye," he says, somehow keeping a straight face.

I laugh. "You're crazy, you know that?"

He grins and continues fishing, but I find myself thinking more about what he said. "You know, there's something else that treats people the same no matter looks or money."

"Oh yeah. What?"

"A dog. I hope my parents let us get one again sometime soon."

"That would be cool."

The fog moves in then, wrapping around us like a blanket. I look down to see loose stone and dirt under my feet. I'm not by Clover Creek anymore, but standing on the side of the road. I can't see, but I feel Charlie next to me—and then the black metal streaks by, ripping Charlie away.

I start running. I slip in the gravel, lose my balance, and

fall down the embankment. I scramble back to my feet. Prick-
ers grab at my legs, biting, trying to trap me, wanting to slow
me down. I kick and thrash. I won't stop. I can't stop. I need
to get help.

I kick and thrash harder, struggling to free my legs. And
then I run. I run and run until I feel the wet fog against my
neck and cheek, and soft whimpers reach me through the mist.

It was dark out, and late, when I stirred awake to find
Jack-Jack still by my side, pressed against me. His soft
cries told me he knew, and his gentle kisses told me it
was okay now. I squeezed him tight, burying my face in
his fur. We stayed like that until Jack lifted his head and
looked toward the door.

"Thanks, buddy," Dad whispered. "She could use a
best friend, so you take care of her for me."

Jack's tail thumped lightly against the bed. I heard
Dad sigh and then turn and walk back downstairs. I swallowed against the knot in my throat.

Jack-Jack never spent another night in his crate
after that.

23

THE MYSTERY BOX SET-UP

I was up early the next morning, already in a sour mood. I'd gone to bed without any dinner, so I was a bit hangry. It didn't help any when the first thing I spotted after venturing downstairs was Abby's mystery box sitting on the floor near the front door. Most likely, Mom had told Abby to leave it there so she didn't forget it. If Mom had been listening last night, she would've known there was no chance of that happening. Abby was beyond excited. But Mom hadn't been listening because she didn't care— not about any box or my sisters' problems with Simon. My blood began to boil all over again.

I left the box and began rummaging through our cabinets, looking for something to eat. Jack-Jack hadn't left my side since getting out of bed until now. Instead of following me into the kitchen he stayed by the door doing the pee-pee dance.

It was times like this when I appreciated our fenced-in backyard most. All I had to do was open the door and let him go. There was none of that walking him at the crack of dawn or late at night, or worse, in the cold or rain—at least, that was how it was supposed to be. Jack had a different idea that morning.

The second I pulled the door open, he grabbed Abby's mystery box and dashed outside with it. Of all the things to take, he had to pick that! He was going to ruin it! I stuck my feet in Dad's boots and thundered after him.

The sun wasn't even up yet and Jack-Jack thought it was playtime. He raced around the backyard with the mystery box still in his mouth. I stomped across the grass, huffing and puffing like the big bad wolf. Miraculously, when Jack saw that I wasn't amused, he dropped the box. I hurried to get it, breathing a sigh of relief. Other than Abby's turtle figurine spilling out, which must've been what she'd chosen to hide, there wasn't any damage. I pocketed the turtle and grabbed the box.

Meanwhile, Jack did his thing. He sniffed here and there until he finally found an acceptable spot. I looked away, giving my dog some privacy when I saw him go into his squat. I started back toward the house. Taking my eye off him was a mistake. Just when I thought all the excitement was behind us, my naughty dog came running, snatched the box from my hand, and took off with it again. Apparently, he wasn't done playing. Well, I was.

I ran after him, growling like a bear. To my surprise, Jack wasn't interested in playing chase or tag. He stopped as soon as he reached his fresh pile of dog doo. I will say this, for a young guy Jack-Jack could produce some monster turds. I had to wonder if our mystery dog wasn't actually part rhinoceros. I should've wondered more about the mystery part, because Jack was all of that. But it took me a while to see that—and longer to believe it.

Jack placed Abby's mystery box on the ground and stood there, staring deep into me. You could say that what ended up inside the box was Jack's idea. Thinking back on it now, I get chills.

24

THE MYSTERY BOX FALLOUT

When Mom showed up at the middle school and yanked me out of class early, I knew there was trouble. I met her in the office. She didn't say a word when I walked in, and she didn't have to; everything I needed to know was written on her face. She shot me a hard glare and then stormed out.

I tucked my tail between my legs and followed. Expecting her to march straight out to our car, I was surprised when instead she turned the corner and decided to first pay Ms. Riley a visit. Mom didn't even knock. Just barged right in.

Ms. Riley was more than slightly startled by the crazed woman charging into her office unannounced. "M-m-may I help you?" she stammered.

"I'm Susan Ettinger, Thea's mother."

"Oh, it's nice to—" Ms. Riley began as she went to get up.

"Don't bother," Mom said, cutting her off. "You can stay in your seat. This won't take long."

Ms. Riley sat back down. She'd gone from startled to intimidated. And Mom was just warming up.

"I appreciate you checking in on my daughter, and I understand you were only trying to do your job," Mom said, "but Thea doesn't want to talk. If that changes, she'll be sure to let you know. I thought I'd made that clear with Principal Starmer when we moved here, but apparently not, so let me make it clear now: if any other adult mentions or tries to talk to Thea about what you noted in her file, I'll be back with my lawyer."

Ms. Riley could only nod.

"Good," Mom said. "Have a nice day." And with that she turned and out the door we went.

I had just witnessed a first-class butt kicking. Inside my head I was yelling to the world, *You mess with me and you mess with my mother!* I wanted to hug her, but Mom was in no mood for celebrating. As soon as we climbed into the car and closed the doors, she unloaded on me.

"Do you know what Abby did today?"

I shook my head while staring at the floor.

"Really? Let me fill you in, then. It seems your sister decided it'd be a good idea to hide dog poop in the mystery box."

I didn't move. I didn't want to give Mom any sort of a reaction.

"This morning, a nice little boy reached his hand in

there and gave the hidden object a good squeeze," Mom continued, acting out parts of the story as she retold it.

"Was it Simon?" The question slipped from my mouth before I could stop it. I had to know.

Mom stopped and stared at me. "What?" she asked, clearly shocked that I'd said anything.

"Was it Simon?" I whispered, continuing to stare at my feet.

"It was," she answered, her voice low.

My smirk broke Mom's spell. It didn't matter that I'd just spoken for the second time in two days after months of silence. She was fuming.

"Thea, let me be clear here. I don't care if that boy has been picking on your sisters. Your stunt crossed the line. That poor little boy started screaming and crying when he realized what he'd done. And then he tried to wipe his hands on the boy next to him."

I grimaced.

"Thank goodness Ms. Stacy stopped him before that happened," Mom went on, "but she wasn't able to stop him from wiping it on his own pants."

Eww, I thought. Dog-poop pants.

"Poor Ms. Stacy really had a mess to deal with. A disaster."

I shrugged.

"No biggie, huh? Then it shouldn't be any big deal for you to go in and apologize."

"What?" I croaked.

"You will be going in and apologizing to Ms. Stacy tomorrow after school. I just hope this Simon boy's parents don't make a stink—no pun intended. I don't want to see your sister get suspended."

"Can't I just write Ms. Stacy a note?" I pleaded.

"No," Mom snapped. "That is not good enough. You got yourself into this mess. Now you have to accept the consequences. And you better apologize to your sister. Ms. Stacy said it was obvious Abby had no idea. She was confused and upset."

I swallowed. I hadn't been nervous or scared up to this point, but now I was terrified.

25

MYSTERY BOX APOLOGY

I spent that night sitting on my bed, writing my apology inside a card while my partner in crime curled up next to me. I told Jack he had to stay because he wasn't innocent in all this, not that he objected. He never left my side. I figured I could hand-deliver the note to Ms. Stacy and avoid needing to talk to her—and Mom would never know the difference. It was a solid plan, but as I was just beginning to see, nothing went as planned since Jack entered my life.

The playground at Johnny Arena Elementary was conveniently located behind Ms. Stacy's classroom, so Liv and Abby kept busy out there while they waited for me to do what I had to after school the next day.

The door was open, but I still knocked. Ms. Stacy looked up from the student desk she was wiping clean.

"Can I help you?"

I swallowed and opened my mouth, but no words came out.

"You must be Thea."

I nodded.

"Livvy and Abby mentioned that you might be dropping by."

I forced one of those no-teeth cheek smiles, and then I quickly held out my card for her—but she didn't take it.

"Come in and have a seat," she said. "I want to show you something."

Ms. Stacy turned and walked to a table on the other side of the room, where she began digging through a stack of notebooks. I thought about dropping my card and taking off, but I worried Mom might hear about it if I did that, so I sucked it up and stayed. I sat in the chair at the closest desk. When Ms. Stacy had Liv and Abby's notebooks she came and sat across from me.

"I've been reading the book *Wish* by Barbara O'Connor to the children," she said. "It's a story about a young girl wishing for something important, and finding a dog and much more along the way. You can bet your sisters were excited about the dog and have had much to say about Jack-Jack."

I smiled—unforced this time. It was small and fleeting, but it happened.

"Is Jack doing any better with the crate?" Ms. Stacy asked.

I shook my head.

"I'd say you should try letting him out, but from what I understand, your father won't go for that."

I shook my head again.

"Well, I'd keep trying," Ms. Stacy said. "Fathers can be stubborn, and it sounds to me like your dog doesn't want to be trapped."

I nodded.

"Well, anyway, to go along with the book we've been reading," Ms. Stacy continued, "I've had the children writing about wishes. This is what I wanted to show you."

Ms. Stacy opened Abby's notebook and slid it in front of me. I looked down and read:

I wish Thea cud be happy agin.
I wish Thea wuznt sad all the time.

I swallowed. Ms. Stacy slid Liv's notebook over next.

I wish I knew how to make Thea all better.
I wish to have my big sister back again.
I wish Thea didn't think the axident was her fallt.

I fought the tightening in my throat, refusing to cry. I choked back another swallow and wiped my eyes. I wished those things too.

"You've got two wonderful little sisters, Thea. I just wanted you to know that they love you very much."

I still had my head down, but I nodded.

"And here they come now," Ms. Stacy said. "And they have a dog."

What? I sat up. Liv and Abby came running up to the classroom window, squealing and laughing.

"Jack-Jack came to play!" Liv yelled through the glass. My mouth fell open.

"Did you go home all by yourselves to get him?" Ms. Stacy asked, sounding concerned.

"Nope. He just showed up," Abby said. "He missed us."

But how? I wondered.

"Looks like you've got yourselves a regular Houdini dog," Ms. Stacy said.

She was right about that. Somehow our dog had not only escaped from his crate, but also our house. How? I continued to wonder, utterly dumbfounded.

"I must have something that we can use for a temporary leash," Ms. Stacy said, rummaging through her closet. "Yes, this should work." She pulled out a bundle of clothesline. "Let's go help your sisters."

I followed her outside. When Jack saw us, he came running, wagging his tail.

"This is Jack-Jack," Liv and Abby told Ms. Stacy.

"It's nice to finally meet you, Mr. Jack-Jack," Ms. Stacy replied. "I've heard a lot about you."

Abby giggled.

"He's a good boy," Livvy said, patting his head.

Just then it started to rain. It was light, but the sky didn't look promising. Wet roads were dangerous. I could feel my anxiety level rising.

"Oh no, we're gonna get soaked," Abby whined.

"I'll give you a ride," Ms. Stacy said. "Don't worry. I just need a minute to get my things together."

"Yay," Liv and Abby cheered.

"Ms. Stacy, you're the best," Abby said.

"Well, I don't know about that, but I'm certainly not going to let two of my finest students walk home in a downpour, even if they are accompanied by their big sister and special dog."

Liv and Abby beamed. We followed Ms. Stacy inside, but stayed near the exit doors while we waited for her to round up her belongings because we had Jack and didn't know if he could be inside the building. It didn't take Ms. Stacy long and then she showed us out to her car.

My sisters climbed into the back with Jack and I hopped in the front. It was a short ride, but it saved us from getting drenched because Ms. Stacy had been right. By the time we reached our house, the light rain had turned into a heavy downpour.

My sisters thanked their teacher and then jumped out and ran inside with Jack-Jack.

"Thea, I'm not sure you ever got to do what you came for today, so I guess I'll be seeing you again," Ms. Stacy said.

My fingers gripped the apology card inside my pocket. I could've given it to her then and been done with this—but I didn't. Instead, I nodded. Then I got out and hurried into the house. I closed the door behind me and stood there thinking. It wasn't that Ms. Stacy needed me to say anything. She was just giving me a reason to go back—in case I wanted to, which I did.

26

FREE!

Liv and Abby told all about Jack's incredible day at dinner that night. Not only did Jack manage to escape his crate, he then proceeded to get out of the house by pushing his way past the screen in the bathroom window. (Mom had left the window open because Jack didn't smell like roses after a day-long slobber-fest inside his crate.) Most amazing of all, once outside, Jack went and found my sisters at school. We had no way to explain that, but Liv and Abby had fun sharing their different theories.

"I think he sniffed our feet tracks," Abby suggested.

"I think he picked up our scent on the wind," Liv said.

"I think the squirrels and birdies told him where to go," Abby said next, getting creative.

"I think he heard us on the playground," Liv decided, which actually might've been the case.

Mom laughed and shook her head while Dad sat in stunned silence. He'd been rendered speechless for all of dinner. He simply couldn't believe what he was hearing. Mom, on the other hand, had heard enough.

"Can we please be done with the crate now?" she asked.

Still no response from my dumbfounded father.

"Please, Daddy," Abby pleaded.

"Please," Livvy echoed.

Dad sighed. "Well, the vet said she'd give us a round of meds to try, but okay. We need to close all of the bedroom and bathroom doors. I don't want to give Jackson free rein over the entire house in case this backfires . . . but we can try leaving him out on Monday."

"Yay!" Liv and Abby cheered.

Jack's tail wagged. He gave Dad's hand a lick.

"This is your big chance, buddy," Dad told him. "Don't blow it."

"He won't," Abby promised—and she was right.

"Jack-Jack's free. Free!" Livvy sang.

More tail wagging.

"Thank goodness," Mom murmured. "It only took all of September."

27

WHITMAN FOREST

Jack-Jack and I were up and at it early the next day. The weekend was here, and with it a batch of beautiful weather. Based on our regular routines, Jack knew when it was and wasn't a school day, and on the non–school days we always dedicated a chunk of our morning to training, which he liked. At this point, Jack had *sit* and *stay* mastered, and he was pretty good at *come* whenever I whistled. Now we were working on *roll over* and *shake*.

We had a good morning, and then just like he did after our first training session, Jack-Jack insisted we go for a walk when we finished up. I didn't mind, but before leaving I decided to throw some treats and a sandwich and an apple into my backpack, just in case we found a good spot for a picnic lunch while we were out and about.

Mom and Dad had mentioned Whitman Forest, a nearby reservation with over thirty acres of hiking trails, when we first moved to the area. At the time I didn't care, nor did I think I'd ever care, but things were different with

Jack-Jack. The forest sounded like the kind of place he might like. So instead of making the familiar trek toward school, we headed in the other direction—and I'm glad we did.

The reservation was beautiful. Jack and I studied the map at the entrance and decided to give the yellow trail a try since a portion of it traveled along a lake that was also part of the reserve. At first, I kept Jack on his leash, but after three squirrels he'd almost pulled my arm off. We were in the middle of the woods, so I didn't have to worry about cars, and like I said, Jack-Jack was pretty good at listening to my whistle, so I decided to let him run free.

He loved it. He ran all over the place chasing chipmunks and squirrels, jumping over logs and darting around trees like a slalom skier. I was smiling before I even realized it, but the best was yet to come.

We were about a mile along when the trail turned down a hill and the lake first came into view, precisely where a colorful group of ducks had congregated not far from shore. The second Jack spotted them he bounded ahead and launched into the water, belly-flop style. It was anything but graceful. A chorus of quacks filled the air followed by a string of big barks. And then it happened. I laughed. For the first time since the accident, I laughed. And it felt good. But my firsts didn't stop there.

As I watched Jack paddling through the water, chasing after those ducks that he had no chance of catching, I felt something else that hadn't been there in a long time. I was hit by a sudden urge. I dug through my backpack until I found my journal. Even though I hadn't opened it since that day, I also hadn't taken it out of my bag. I pulled out my colored pencils next, and then I sat on a nearby log. I flipped through the pages, stopping on the last sketch I'd made, a drawing of a dragonfly I'd seen perched on a rock at Clover Creek. I studied it, remembering that day, and exhaled. I looked out at Jack-Jack, jumping and splashing in the shallows, trying to catch the little minnows he'd spotted now. I smiled. Then I turned to a clean page and began drawing.

After Jack was done tormenting the fish and the ducks had swum off, he shook the water from his fur and lay down by my side. There had been a lot of excited chatter and celebration at dinner the night before, but I never said anything. Instead, my words came out during the small meal Jack and I shared by the water's edge.

"I want to go and see Ms. Stacy again," I confessed, "but I don't think I can."

Jack lifted his head and looked at me. He was listening. He always listened to me.

"What would I even say to her?" I asked.

I didn't expect him to answer, but I knew he understood. He'd helped me with Simon and the mystery box, so maybe he'd help me again.

I was right. The opportunity presented itself a week later when Livvy came home with Snowball, her class's beloved stuffed bunny. Sometimes sacrifices are needed for a greater good.

PART III

28

BUNNY ATTACK

Jack-Jack was perfect without his crate. No barking. No destruction. No nothing. Just one happy pup. My father still couldn't believe that was all it took.

"You live and learn, I guess" was all he could say.

While Jack's crate situation was finally settled, things in my life were not. Mom seemed satisfied the apology had happened, but I still wanted to go and see Ms. Stacy again, except I didn't have the courage, and now that it had been a week since my first visit to her classroom, I didn't think I could go back. But I wanted to. And I wasn't even sure I could tell you why. I just did.

The good news: Jack-Jack was fully aware of my ongoing dilemma. It was thanks to him that I'd met Ms. Stacy in the first place, and it was thanks to him that I found a reason to visit a second time.

Livvy came home with Snowball on Friday, and boy, was she excited. Abby too! Livvy had to write about Snowball's many adventures with our family in the bunny's journal that traveled with her from home to home. I doubt you'll be surprised to hear me say my sisters had so much planned. What a weekend that bunny had!

First up was a fancy tea party that the family—Jack included—had to attend to officially welcome Snowball to our home. Jack was a good boy and never once showed interest in Snowball. He pretended to be more concerned with the tiny carrots my sisters served. He had us fooled.

The next day began with a special breakfast featuring French toast and—you guessed it—carrots. That was followed by an afternoon picnic and then movie night to cap things off. It wasn't even close to Easter yet, but my sisters decided to watch *Hop* because they thought Snowball would enjoy a movie that featured a bunny.

Jack let my sisters have their fun, patiently waiting for his opening. Come Sunday night, he got his chance. Liv and Abby must have lost interest in Snowball. Either that, or they were exhausted from their many weekend adventures. Whatever the reason, the bunny was left on the couch, unattended, when they went to bed.

I couldn't tell you how long it took, but I'm sure it happened fast. I came out of the bathroom and walked into the living room to find Jack standing over a pile of stuffie guts. Snowball's ear was ripped off and her butt torn open.

I gasped. Jack-Jack snatched the furball and streaked upstairs. I bent down and quickly scooped up Snowball's insides. If Liv and Abby found out about this, there would be a major meltdown. Like, major.

I didn't have a clue what I was going to do, but I knew it started with me finding my dog before there was nothing left of Snowball. I raced upstairs after him.

As expected, I found the naughty culprit in my bedroom. He slunk under my bed and crawled behind my box of Charlie stuff. The box I wasn't sure I'd ever open again—until now.

29

WEDDING BELLS

Mom had the same reaction as me when she walked into my bedroom and spotted a gutted Snowball. "Ahh!" she gasped in horror.

"Jackson," Dad growled, glaring at my guilty dog.

I pulled Roscoe, the bunny I'd won thanks to Charlie, from behind my back and held him out.

"Where did you get that?" Mom asked.

I pointed to my box of Charlie stuff.

"Oh yes, I remember now. You came home with him in first grade."

I nodded.

"Well, it's not exactly the same, but it should work," Dad said.

"Are you kidding? It'll never work," Mom argued. "That bunny looks nothing like Snowball. The girls will definitely know."

"Who's Snowball?" Dad asked.

"Oh my God," Mom groaned. "Snowball is the name

of their class pet, the dead bunny over there. Were you or were you not at the tea party?"

"Oh."

"Yeah, 'oh,'" Mom mimicked, shaking her head.

"I've been thinking," I said, taking my parents by surprise. They still weren't used to me talking much. "What if we say the new bunny is Snowball's boyfriend?"

Mom looked at Dad and shrugged. "Okay," she said. "But that still doesn't explain why Snowball is dead."

"The butler did it," Dad suggested.

"No!" Mom shrieked. "These are little kids. We're not turning this into one of your detective shows."

Dad shrugged. "I thought it was good."

"I've got it!" Mom said. "Snowball's gone dress shopping. For her wedding to—"

"Roscoe," I said.

"To Roscoe," Mom finished. "That buys us a day to find a replacement."

"I can go to the mall when I get off work tomorrow," Dad offered.

"No, I'll go," Mom insisted. "I need to make sure we get an exact replica. Knowing you, you'd come back with a stuffed elephant and try to pass that off as Snowball."

Dad shrugged again, knowing that didn't sound so far-fetched.

"Now we just need to convince Liv and Abby that everything is fine tomorrow morning," Mom said, "and we also need to tell Ms. Stacy the real story."

"I'll tell her," I volunteered.

Jack's tail wagged.

"You want to go and explain this to her?" Mom asked, making sure she understood.

"Yes," I replied.

"Okay. I'll send a note in with your sisters telling Ms. Stacy she should expect you after school, and that you'll explain about Snowball then."

I nodded and Jack-Jack's tail wagged faster.

"And, Thea," Mom said, pausing in my doorway before leaving, "it's nice to see some of your drawings again. They're really terrific."

I glanced at the mallard duck I'd tacked up after my day with Jack at Whitman Forest. "Thanks."

Mom smiled, then turned and left. I rubbed Jack-Jack's side and we got ready for bed. I had a big day ahead of me.

30

EXPLAINING THE IMPOSTER

The first part was easy. Liv and Abby thought it was great that Snowball had found a boyfriend and was getting married. They couldn't wait to take Roscoe into school to tell their classmates the big news. Talk about gullible.

It was the next part of the plan that wasn't so easy. I spent all day thinking about what to say to Ms. Stacy. I'd told my parents that I'd go and explain, but now I was having second thoughts. Was I really going to be able to talk to her? Other than Jack-Jack and my family, no one had heard my voice since the accident.

I walked into Johnny Arena Elementary, my heart pounding harder with every step that brought me closer to Ms. Stacy's classroom. I was so consumed by nerves and doubt that I wasn't paying attention to anything else. I never even saw the boy until he was there. Standing in front of me. Talking.

"Hey, are you the one who fixed the mystery box with dog poop?"

I jumped.

"Sorry. I didn't mean to scare you. But was that you?"

I froze, staring at the floor.

"It was you. You're dog-poop girl!" he exclaimed, sounding proud of his discovery.

Who was this boy?

"I go to the middle school, but I heard all about it because my mom is the principal here. I think it's awesome. That Simon terror has taken years off my mom's life. It's about time somebody taught him a lesson."

I don't know what made me, but I glanced up at him and he smiled. I quickly looked away again.

"Hi, Rory," a familiar voice said as someone approached us. It was Ms. Stacy. "I see you've met Thea."

"Yup," he replied. "Had to meet the legend."

Ms. Stacy laughed. "I'm quite certain you're a legend too," she said.

"Yeah," he scoffed. "The bulletin-board legend, maybe."

"Rory is a big help around here," Ms. Stacy explained. "He's responsible for all the bulletin boards you see in the lobby and main hallway. As you can see, he's very creative."

I nodded to be polite but didn't dare look at him again.

"Well, I'm on my way to the library to do a little homework while I wait for Mom," he said. "Nice meeting you, Thea. I'll see you later, Ms. Stacy."

"See you later," she replied.

Rory went one way and I followed Ms. Stacy in the

opposite direction. Don't ask me why, but before turning the corner, I glanced back. Rory caught me peeking and waved. I darted behind the wall, ready to die—but it wasn't like I was safe, because now came the thing I'd been worrying about all day. It was time for me to talk to Ms. Stacy.

"Your sisters are out on the playground," she explained when we entered her classroom. "I told them we'd come and find them in a little bit."

I nodded.

"Have a seat," she said, and gestured.

I chose the same desk I'd sat in the first time. Ms. Stacy took the seat across from me again.

"Your mother sent in a note explaining what happened with Snowball. You've got quite the dog there, Thea."

I nodded. (We still didn't know the half of it.)

"The kids loved Roscoe and the wedding story," Ms. Stacy said, "so I'm not too concerned. But tell me, Thea, wherever did you find another bunny on such short notice?"

This was it. I swallowed. "I had it," I croaked.

Ms. Stacy waited, giving me the chance to say more.

I swallowed again. "My friend helped me win it from the prize box in first grade."

"Helped you win it? How's that?" Ms. Stacy asked, curious.

"We had to guess how many jelly beans were in Mrs. Hobby's jar. The closest person got to pick out of the prize box. Charlie—"

I stopped. My hand flew to my lips, covering my mouth.

Again, Ms. Stacy waited. If I'd shut down and quit talking she would've been fine with it—but I didn't.

I took a breath. "Charlie saw where Mrs. Hobby had written down the answer and told me," I finished, letting go of the air I was holding.

Ms. Stacy smiled. A warm smile. "Good friend," she said.

"The best."

We were quiet for a moment before Ms. Stacy spoke again. "Do you mind if I ask you another question, Thea?"

"No." It was funny how after being mute for so long, talking happened naturally once I got started. It wasn't as if I'd forgotten how, I just chose not to. But I liked talking with Ms. Stacy.

"The mystery box," she said.

"Yeah, I still need to apologize for that."

"How in the world did you think of that one?" she asked.

I shifted in my chair. I didn't tell her about Jack-Jack. Instead I told her about Charlie.

"When we were in second grade, we had a boy named Fred in our class," I began. "I think Fred was a lot like Simon, only meaner."

"Simon's a sweet boy," Ms. Stacy said. "He struggles with self-control and personal space, but he's been doing better since your lesson," she added, and smirked.

I grinned. "Fred was especially mean to Charlie," I continued. "He was always making fun of Charlie's lazy eye."

"A lazy eye, like Jack-Jack?" Ms. Stacy mused.

"Yes," I replied. "Fred liked to call Charlie a pirate and stuff like that. Charlie pretended not to care, so then Fred started stealing his lunch, rummaging through it and taking whatever he wanted."

I paused then and looked at Ms. Stacy.

She sat forward. "Charlie put dog poop in his lunch?" she asked, almost sounding excited.

I giggled. "No, but he did switch out his usual PB&J sandwich for a peanut butter and worm special. You should've seen it when Fred stole that thing and took a big juicy bite! Boy, did he freak. He spit it all over the floor and started screaming and crying like a big baby.

"Fred was sent to the nurse and Charlie had to see the principal, but he didn't get in much trouble and Fred left Charlie alone after that, so we both agreed it was worth it."

Ms. Stacy sat back and smiled. "I like Charlie," she said.

"He was great."

We stayed there for a minute, thinking our own thoughts, and then I told Ms. Stacy I should round up my sisters and get going. Jack would be waiting for us, looking out the living room window and wondering where we were.

Ms. Stacy nodded. "See you later," she said when I got up from my chair.

"See you later," I replied—and I knew I would.

31

HIPPO FACE

Another week passed, bringing us into the middle of October. I barely had any homework so Jack-Jack and I worked on training and spent another afternoon at Whitman Forest—at his request—where he got to swim and romp while I sat and sketched a blue heron that stalked the shallows nearby, and then it was "later."

Mom still felt terrible and partly responsible for the whole Snowball fiasco, so she decided to put together a little something for Ms. Stacy. It wasn't much, just a few candles and lotions and some chocolates tucked into a gift bag, but the candles were in glass jars so they were fragile and the lotions could open and make a mess, so Mom asked if I'd be willing to deliver it after school because she didn't trust my sisters. More importantly, she'd finally tracked down a replacement for the original Snowball—wedding-dress shopping took longer than expected—so she needed me to deliver the new bunny as well. She didn't have to ask me twice.

The only problem I foresaw was the fact that I couldn't stuff the gift bag inside my backpack without ruining it and I didn't feel like carrying it to school—and I definitely wasn't bringing a stuffed bunny to middle school!—so I decided I'd simply run home after I got out to quickly grab everything before going to get Liv and Abby. It was a good plan, but once I walked into the house, I realized I'd failed to think of something.

Jack-Jack was there to greet me the moment I stepped inside the door, tail wagging and body shaking with excitement. He was so happy to see me. I couldn't turn around and leave him again—not when I just got home. I had no choice but to bring him with me. I put him on his leash, grabbed the gift bag and bunny that I'd come for, and out the door we went. Ms. Stacy wouldn't mind. Besides, Jack-Jack was the one who really needed to say sorry for the original Snowball's destruction.

I wish I could say the walk to Arena Elementary was easy and uneventful, but that wasn't the case. At that time of day there were school buses and trucks everywhere. Each time one came roaring by, Jack-Jack cowered and yanked at his leash, desperate to get as far away as possible. This was his normal behavior, and I was used to it, but more than once I almost dropped those fragile candles. Ask me and I would've said it was a miracle we made it with everything still in one piece—but then again, I didn't know anything about real miracles just yet.

Liv and Abby knew the plan so they hung out with Ms. Stacy until I got there. I waited until the crowd in front of Johnny Arena dispersed and then I went to Ms. Stacy's back windows and knocked. Liv and Abby were so thrilled to see I had Jack-Jack with me that they came running outside. They took him to the playground while I went inside to deliver Mom's gift—and the new Snowball, which my sisters didn't know about.

"This bunny is perfect," Ms. Stacy said. "The children will be so excited to see Snowball again." She turned to me. "Thea, please tell your mother I said thank you, but this other stuff was wholly unnecessary. She's too kind."

I smiled and watched as Ms. Stacy opened her bag, pulling out the different items. I already knew what was inside, but it's fun to see how people react to presents. Needless to say, I wasn't really paying attention to anything else, so the sudden knock startled me. I jumped, banging my knees on the underside of the desk, and quickly twisted around.

It was Rory. He walked into the classroom performing an array of movements with his hands and fingers. He stopped when he was near me. Noticing my puzzled expression, he explained, "It's sign language. I just said 'Sorry. I didn't mean to scare you.' Do you happen to know sign language?"

I was familiar with a few different gestures—the thumbs-up, for example, and Mom's personal favorite, my eye roll—but that was the extent of my knowledge. Of course, I didn't share this with Rory. On the contrary, I didn't give him any response.

He wasn't deterred; he came prepared. Rory slipped off his backpack and pulled out a book that he slid onto my desk. You guessed it; it was a book about sign language.

"If you study up, I thought maybe you and I could talk? With our hands and not our mouths," he added to clarify, though that wasn't necessary.

I glimpsed Ms. Stacy smiling. She thought this was cute. I squirmed in my chair.

"But if you don't want to talk to me, that's okay," Rory continued. "There's also a few chapters on using sign language to communicate with your pet that you might find interesting. I've seen you walking your dog," he confessed. "But I already kinda knew you must have a dog since you booby trapped the mystery box with dog poop. Anyway, animal trainers have used sign with dogs, dolphins, tigers, horses . . . all sorts of creatures," he finished in a rush.

When I still didn't respond, Ms. Stacy filled the silence for us—and I bet Rory wished she hadn't. "That's very thoughtful of you, Rory."

Rory's face turned redder than a tomato. And then something happened I wasn't expecting. I giggled. Rory's eyes brightened, and then he smiled—a sheepish smile because he was still embarrassed.

That special awkward moment came to an abrupt end when Abby came banging on the back window. "Jack-Jack's a bulldog!" she squealed.

My face scrunched. What was she talking about? I rose from my chair and went to see.

Abby was wrong. Jack didn't look like a bulldog. He had a full-blown hippo face. His eyebrows and lips were extra puffy.

"Does your dog always look like that?" Rory asked, standing next to me.

"No," Ms. Stacy answered. I heard the concern in her voice, and rightfully so. "Thea, I think he's having an allergic reaction. We need to get him to a vet."

True, but we didn't have that much time. I could see Jack-Jack taking short rapid breaths, already struggling to breathe. I grabbed my backpack and raced outside. Rory and Ms. Stacy weren't far behind. I ran and slid on the grass next to my dog and dug through my stuff. Where was it? Frantic, I flipped my bag over and dumped everything out. Wrappers, papers, coins, rubber bands, headphones, all sorts of junk spilled onto the ground— including the one thing I was looking for.

I snatched the EpiPen and stabbed it in Jack-Jack's upper leg. He let out a whimper.

"What're you doing?" Livvy shrieked, scared and confused.

"Don't hurt Jack-Jack!" Abby shouted.

"It's all right," Ms. Stacy assured my sisters. "Jack-Jack's having an allergic reaction. The shot will help, but we've got to get him to a vet."

I threw everything back into my bag and got to my feet. Rory lifted Jack and carried him to Ms. Stacy's car.

I opened the back door and Rory slid him onto the seat. I hurried around to the passenger's side while my sisters piled inside next to Jack. Rory closed the door behind them and stepped back out of the way. Ms. Stacy started the engine and put it in drive.

I saw Rory's concerned face in my side mirror as we disappeared from sight.

32

CLOSE CALL

"Most likely, Jack got stung by something and that's what caused his allergic reaction," said Dr. Sandra, the vet. "Or maybe he ate something?" she offered as another possibility and shrugged. "It's hard to know for sure, but what I can tell you is that you saved your dog today," she stressed, looking me square in the face. "If you hadn't used that EpiPen, I don't know if he would've made it."

I swallowed and glanced away.

"Is Jack-Jack going to be okay?" Abby asked.

"Yes," Dr. Sandra answered. "I've spoken to your mom. We're going to keep Jack here for a few hours, just to monitor his recovery, but you should be able to take him home later tonight."

My sisters smiled.

"One of the receptionists can give you my business card on the way out. You can call if you want to check in on how Jack's doing, but the plan is for your mom or dad to get in touch in a few hours and then we'll coordinate a pickup time."

"Thank you," Ms. Stacy said.

"You're welcome," Dr. Sandra replied. "Bye, girls."

Ms. Stacy drove us home after that. Liv and Abby thanked their teacher and said goodbye, and then they hopped out and raced inside—same as always—but I stayed frozen in the passenger's seat.

Ms. Stacy must have sensed I wanted to talk, but I was having a hard time starting. "Your sisters are getting excited for Halloween," she said, breaking the ice after a long minute of silence.

"Charlie wasn't a fan of trick-or-treating," I replied. "He liked the costumes and jack-o'-lanterns and all, but the actual trick-or-treating part made no sense to him. If you think about it, he was right. I mean, we go up to a random door and say trick or treat like it's a question, but the person doesn't answer, just gives us candy instead. It's pretty ridiculous."

Ms. Stacy chuckled. "When you say it like that, I guess it doesn't make much sense," she agreed.

"Nope. Charlie sure didn't think so. He was always really curious about everything, so he did some research and discovered that in other parts of the world, people actually performed tricks or sang songs before receiving a treat."

"Really?" Ms. Stacy said.

"Yup. Charlie reasoned the original phrase must've

been trick-*for*-treat, and that the 'f' in 'for' had gotten lost along the way—so he made it his goal to bring it back. He was so determined that he even gave up going out to get candy and stayed home so that when kids came to his door, he could teach them the proper phrase and then make them perform a trick, sing a song, recite a poem, or do anything entertaining before giving them a treat."

"Did it work?" Ms. Stacy asked.

"Not at first," I admitted, "but Charlie didn't waver, and once a few kids joined in the fun and word spread, his house became a favorite."

"Didn't he miss not getting candy?"

"No, I always went out early because of my sisters, and when I got done I joined Charlie and shared my loot with him."

Ms. Stacy laughed. "What a team."

I smiled and nodded, and then we grew quiet again. But Ms. Stacy waited, somehow knowing I'd find the courage to keep going if she was patient.

"It was Charlie's EpiPen," I finally said.

"I guessed as much," Ms. Stacy replied, her voice low.

"He had a close call in third grade when he got stung during recess. I went with him to the nurse's office to get an ice pack to put on the sting, and by the time we got there his lips had begun to swell and he started having difficulty breathing. I'd never seen anything like that before, but Mrs. Olson, our nurse, she knew what was happening. She stuck Charlie with an EpiPen from the emergency kit and immediately called the ambulance.

It was really scary . . . but I've seen worse." My voice trailed off.

I almost told Ms. Stacy about the accident then, but something stopped me. I couldn't. Not yet. So I told her more about Charlie instead.

"Charlie was an only child and he had much older parents. His mom and dad were told they couldn't have children—and they didn't for many years—but then they got a big surprise when Charlie came along."

"I would think so!" Ms. Stacy exclaimed.

"I always teased Charlie that he was a miracle child."

"Sounds like he was."

I nodded. "After that whole bee-sting scare, his mom asked me to carry an EpiPen. Charlie and I were always together, so his mom figured the best way she could protect him was to have me at the ready. The more people were prepared and aware, the better off he'd be."

"Having you prepared saved Jack-Jack today," Ms. Stacy said.

But not Charlie, I thought. "I better go."

Ms. Stacy put her hand on my arm. "Thea, you don't need a reason to visit. You can come by whenever you want."

I nodded. "Thanks," I said.

"Besides, I'm pretty sure Rory would like that," she teased.

"See you later," I grumbled, and sneered—but it was a fake sneer. Even after all that had happened, Ms. Stacy found a way to send me off with a smile.

33

ROCKETS

I saw Rory at school the next day. In my science class, to be exact. I'd been in school for two months and I'd never noticed him there before. Then again, I couldn't name a single person in that class.

Our teacher, Ready-for-retirement Mr. Morris, had the classroom arranged in rows of single desks and we spent the majority of every day watching videos, so it wasn't like I was looking around at kids. I'd overheard some of my classmates complaining that the class was boring, but it wasn't to me. The structure and routine made it easy to stay hidden and do well—I had a perfect one hundred percent—plus the videos were good.

Today's movie was about gases, which prompted farting sounds from a few of the more immature boys, but I ignored them and continued with my sketches and notes—until I felt somebody staring at me. Have you ever felt that before? When you just know someone is staring?

Slowly, I lifted my gaze and glanced around the room

to see if I was right or just being paranoid. Turns out I was right. I peeked to my left and spotted Rory sitting three desks over, eyes locked on me, like he was waiting for me to look in his direction. I yanked my gaze away faster than you would your hand from a hot stove and returned to my notes—but a few seconds later, I found myself slowly tilting my chin and glancing his way again.

He smiled—big (lots of teeth).

I returned his smile—sheepish (mouth small and closed).

Then Rory did a sign, quick before I looked away again. I knew what it was. I'd gone through his book and studied it a little. It was the sign for dog. He was asking about Jack-Jack. I'd forgotten he was there during all that scary stuff yesterday.

I replied with a simple thumbs-up. Dad could've done without the emergency vet bill, but he and Mom were happy Jack was okay.

Rory smiled again and did some signing back that I assumed meant he was happy to hear that—or something similar.

I signed thank you. (I knew that one.)

More smiling—from Rory and me.

"Your first project," Mr. Morris announced after flipping on the lights.

Wait, what? Project?

"Rockets, like you just saw in today's video," Mr. Morris continued. "You will be designing, building, and testing your own bottle rocket. We will have a special Launch

Day in back of the school at the conclusion. We're out of time for today, but you should start thinking about whether you want to do this work alone or with a partner. No groups of three. I'll share more details and information tomorrow."

Class ended and Rory flashed me one more sign before leaving the classroom. A small wave.

And I felt something I hadn't felt in a long time.

34

SIMON

That afternoon was my first attempt at going to see Ms. Stacy just because. Actually, I had a reason—I had Jack-Jack with me so she could see he was all better, plus I had a gift card for her that Mom had purchased to say thank you for everything—but Ms. Stacy wasn't in her room when I arrived.

My sisters had Jack out on the playground, and I stood among the small desks, hoping that Ms. Stacy had just stepped out to use the bathroom. While waiting for her to return, I ventured over to the stack of notebooks and searched for Liv's and Abby's. I wondered if they'd written anything more about me.

"Ms. Stacy's in a meeting."

The sudden voice was enough to have given an older person a surefire heart attack. I jumped and wheeled around, hands clutching my chest.

It was Rory, sneaking up on me again. "Sorry. I didn't mean to scare you," he said from the doorway.

My scowl was effective sign language. He knew I wasn't buying that.

"No, really," he exclaimed. "Sorry."

I turned my attention back to the notebooks, ignoring him, a response that clearly meant I still wasn't convinced. I wasn't letting him off the hook that easy.

"Ms. Stacy's in a meeting with my mom and Simon's parents," Rory explained, stepping into the classroom. "Simon is on the verge of getting kicked out of the after-school club, and it's not because of anything he did. It's because his parents have been late to pick him up so many times."

My face softened and my shoulders slumped. I looked back at Rory then.

"He has self-control issues and gets in a lot of trouble but, according to Mom, Simon's a good kid. He just wants attention. Mom says his parents are career-driven people and they shouldn't have had a kid in the first place because they never have time for Simon—and they aren't doing a darn thing to help him do any better in school."

I frowned.

"I've said too much," Rory apologized. "I told Mom I'd never repeat those things. Please don't tell anyone."

I lifted one eyebrow, my sign language for—"Really? Are you serious right now?"—because me telling anyone was pretty farfetched.

Rory laughed. "Yeah, guess I don't have to worry about that, huh?" he said, and shrugged, turning red again.

I giggled—and then I nearly died from a second heart attack. The barrage of fists against the windows made Rory jump and yell just as much as me. I spun around to find a young boy with my dog.

"Simon," Rory whispered.

That's Simon, I thought. He didn't look like the little devil I'd been imagining. Actually, he was kinda cute.

"What's he doing out there?" Rory said. "He's supposed to be in after-school club while his parents are in their meeting. He must've snuck away without anyone noticing."

What's he doing with Jack-Jack? I wanted to ask. My question was answered when Abby came running. "Gotcha!" she yelled, tagging the little boy.

"Jack-Jack found me!" Simon squealed.

Livvy joined them next. "Now Abby and I get to hide and you and Jack seek," she said.

"Okay," Simon cheered.

The three of them plus Jack ran off.

"Looks like Simon found some playmates," Rory said, stating the obvious.

Rory and I watched as Simon covered his eyes, and Jack's too, as best he could, and my sisters ran and hid.

"Do you think he knows it was Jack's poop he squeezed inside the mystery box?" Rory asked.

I shrugged. It didn't seem to matter. Simon and Jack-Jack were best buds. When Simon finished counting, he and Jack sprang into action, searching for my sisters.

Their squealing and laughing, along with Jack's happy face and dangling tongue, had me grinning from ear to ear without even realizing it.

"What're you two watching that has you smiling like that?" Ms. Stacy asked, joining us at the windows.

I pointed. Together, we watched another round of hide-and-seek, but that one didn't end so well. A woman, who I assumed was Simon's mother, showed up and stood off to the side, yelling at him.

"It's time to go!"

Naturally, Simon didn't want to listen. He was having too much fun. But the woman didn't have time for that. She stormed onto the playground and grabbed the little boy by his shirtsleeve. It was an ugly scene that I didn't want to witness, so I turned away from the windows.

"I have an idea," Ms. Stacy said.

35

MS. STACY'S IDEA

"I don't know about all of you, but I'm sure glad to be having a normal dinner after last night's excitement," Mom said, taking her seat at the table.

"I'll say. Don't try that again, Jackson," Dad warned.

Jack looked at Dad as if to acknowledge he'd heard him and then put his head back on my foot.

"So, how were your days?" Mom asked.

"Jack-Jack played hide-and-seek with us after school!" Abby exclaimed, unable to keep her news in any longer. Jack perked right up, his tail wagging excitedly. I rubbed his head. "It was so much fun!" Abby cheered. "Jack-Jack was the seeker."

"More like the assistant seeker," Liv clarified. "He stayed with whoever was counting and then went searching when time was up."

"I bet he found you every time," Dad predicted.

"Yup," Abby said.

"Did you play, Thea?" Mom asked out of curiosity.

"Nope. Thea was with Ms. Stacy and Rory," Abby was quick to explain, "but Simon played."

"Simon?" Mom repeated, raising her eyebrows.

"Who's Rory?" Dad asked, narrowing his.

"Thea's boyfriend," Liv replied.

"Really?" Mom said, sounding too excited. She glanced at Dad and smiled.

"No!" I snapped, glaring at my big-mouth sister. I could feel the heat rushing to my face. "Ms. Stacy really appreciated the gift card," I told Mom, trying to change the subject.

"A boyfriend?" Dad repeated, playing his role of the protective father.

I glared at him next.

"Ms. Stacy wants Thea to keep bringing Jack-Jack to school at the end of the day because she wants to make playing with him Simon's reward if he has a good day," Abby explained.

"What?" Mom asked.

"You know how Simon struggles in school," Livvy said, repeating what she'd heard Ms. Stacy say.

"What?" Mom asked again, lost and perplexed.

"You know how Simon struggles in school, right?" Liv repeated, slower this time.

"Yeah, sure," Mom replied, sounding skeptical.

"Well, Ms. Stacy is going to make a special contract with Simon that says if he has a good day and does what he's supposed to, then he gets to play with Jack-Jack after school."

"And she thinks that will work?" Mom asked.

"Yup," Abby said. "Simon's always wanted a doggie but his parents won't let him."

"He loves Jack-Jack," Liv said, which prompted more happy tail wagging.

"And you're willing to hang out with Ms. Stacy while your sisters and Simon play?" Mom asked me.

I nodded, maybe too enthusiastically.

"And Rory too?" Dad pressed.

I glared at him again.

36

WANNA BE MY PARTNER?

I had Jack-Jack with me the next afternoon, anxious to find out if Ms. Stacy's plan had worked. Technically, Simon was still in the after-school club, but Ms. Stacy was willing to give this a try if it made her and everyone else's school day with Simon easier. The big question: Was playing with Jack the perfect motivator for Simon—as Ms. Stacy had predicted? It was time to find out.

Jack and I waited for Arena Elementary to clear out and then we started toward Ms. Stacy's back windows. We didn't make it that far. The moment he saw us approaching Simon burst out the door and came running. "Jack-Jack!" he squealed. Liv and Abby weren't far behind.

Jack-Jack's tail did a million miles an hour. He had three faces to kiss and not just two. He danced at their feet, twirling in between them, soaking up all the attention.

"C'mon, Jack-Jack!" Simon yelled. "We're it!" The

two of them took off running. Simon's laughter bounced across the schoolyard and made my insides melt.

"His day wasn't perfect," Ms. Stacy said, joining me outside, "but it was better. I think now that he sees what his reward really is, he'll try even harder."

I looked at her and smiled. Jack-Jack was helping Simon. Little did we know, before we got done, he would do something even greater.

"Liv and Abby were terrific," Ms. Stacy said. "My two little assistants. They gave Simon gentle reminders of Jack-Jack to keep him on track and following directions throughout the day. I just have to be careful they don't start mothering Simon too much. Nobody wants too many mothers. One is enough."

I laughed. Boy, was she right about that.

Ms. Stacy snickered. "C'mon. Let's go inside while they have their fun."

We left the field and walked back into the school and who do you think we ran into? Yup, you guessed it. Rory.

He waved and I gave a quick wave back, but then I lowered my gaze and studied the floor.

"Hi, Rory," Ms. Stacy said. "What are you up to this afternoon?"

"Time to decorate the bulletin boards with some turkeys. We have Halloween this weekend and then it's November. Mom says Thanksgiving's gonna be here before we know it, which means I need to get it done."

"Well, she's right about that," Ms. Stacy said. "It's only

a few weeks away. You know what they say, time flies when you're having fun."

"Did your plan work? Is Simon outside playing with Jack?" Rory asked.

"Simon is outside with Livvy and Abby and Jack-Jack, playing hide-and-seek," Ms. Stacy replied. "Today was a better day."

"That's great!" he exclaimed.

His genuine and enthusiastic response made me smile and glance at him again. He caught me peeking and smiled back. But then something weird happened. Rory looked away before I did. He was the one studying the floor now, scuffing his foot back and forth.

He cleared his throat. "So Thea, I was wondering . . ." He started slow, but then everything came out in a rush. "You wanna be my partner for our rocket project. I know you still haven't talked to me, but we can use sign language and we see each other a lot and I think we could make a good team."

My whole body tensed. He sounded just like Charlie had with the frogs in first grade. But was he asking or telling? I couldn't respond. I didn't know how. I didn't know the answer.

"I usually do my projects alone," he admitted, "but I thought it'd be fun to have a partner this time."

It was too much. Too soon. Too unexpected. I didn't know what to do—so I ran.

37

IT'S OKAY

I finally started to breathe again when I reached the safety of Ms. Stacy's classroom.

"You weren't ready for that, I take it," Ms. Stacy said when she caught up to me.

I shook my head.

"For what it's worth, I think you should be his partner."

I looked at her with wide eyes.

"What? I think you should."

I turned away. "I can't."

"Why?"

"I just can't."

Ms. Stacy came and stood in front of me then. She grasped me by the shoulders. "Thea, I need you to listen to me. Are you listening?"

I gave a slight nod.

"It's okay for you to make another friend."

I didn't move.

"Do you hear me? It's okay."

I stared at the floor. I didn't want Ms. Stacy to see my eyes watering. I sniffled and tried to steady my breathing. She handed me a tissue. "It's okay," she said again.

I blew my nose and dragged my shirt sleeve across my eyes. "Doesn't Rory have other friends he could ask?"

"Yes, but he's asked you."

"Why?"

Ms. Stacy smiled and shrugged. "Maybe because you're a legend," she said.

I scoffed.

"Thea, Charlie would've liked Rory. I know he would've. Rory is a smart, caring, all-around great kid. Give him a chance."

I blew my nose and wiped my face again. Then I straightened and took a breath. Standing tall and steadying myself, I said, "Okay."

"Okay, what?"

"Okay, I think I'll give Rory a hand with those turkeys."

I could still see Ms. Stacy smiling when I left her classroom.

38

DREAMLAND

I walk down the hall, holding my journal close to my chest. Rory is hard at work on his bulletin board, a hilarious display of turkeys playing football underneath the words HAPPY THANKSGIVING. I let a giggle slip and quickly cover my mouth—but it's too late.

Rory turns and sees me approaching. "It's silly, I know," he says, embarrassed, "but I think the kids will like it."

"I love it," I sign.

Rory smiles.

Slowly, I flip my journal around for him to see. I have the letters OK written across a clean page.

"Okay?" he says, puzzled.

I nod.

His scowl deepens.

I nod again—and then he gets it.

Rory's face brightens. "Okay, you'll be my partner?" he asks hesitantly.

Now I smile. I lower my journal and nod once more.

"Great!" he exclaims.

I place my backpack and journal off to the side and then grab a laminated football helmet from the folder he has sitting on the ground. I pass it to him so that he can put it on one of his turkeys. After he has it attached, I pass him another one—and this time my fingers brush against his. I feel my face burning and stare in the other direction. I step to the side and accidentally kick my journal. It slides across the floor, opening to a different page.

Rory bends to get it for me. "Whoa, Thea. These drawings are amazing," he says. He turns the page, curious to see if I have more, then quickly closes my journal and hands it back to me, suddenly aware that he's being nosy. The only person I'd shared my journal with outside of my family was Charlie—but I am not upset that Rory saw it.

I woke to the warm sun shining on my face and rolled onto my side. Jack-Jack yawned and stretched, pushing his back against my belly. I reached down and gave him a pet. My nightmares had stopped ever since he started sleeping with me, but this was my first happy dream. And the truth was, I didn't know whether I had Jack to thank for it—or Rory.

39

NOVEMBER'S REGULAR ROUTINE

November fell into a regular routine. I would hurry home after school to get Jack and then he and I would leash-walk—with him still cowering and tugging to get away from the buses and other rumbling engines—to Johnny Arena Elementary, where he'd get to play with Simon and my sisters while I worked with Rory on our rocket project.

Simon still wasn't perfect for Ms. Stacy, but his improvement was remarkable. Liv and Abby never complained about him anymore. Not once had he missed out on playing with Jack-Jack. The boy loved our dog—and Jack loved him.

Hide-and-seek was still the favorite game among the group, but they were enjoying a new activity for now. The leaves had begun to fall and there was a section of the schoolyard already covered in them. Ms. Stacy brought in a rake, and they were having a blast pulling the leaves into piles and running and jumping into them—Jack-Jack included, of course.

It was fun to watch, and I got to witness a lot of it because I was outside working on my rocket with Rory. Launch Day was scheduled for the week of Thanksgiving, so we were getting close.

At this point, my sign-language skills had improved enough that Rory and I were able to communicate and work together quite well. It was all thanks to Rory's book and the videos I'd been watching online. What can I say, I wanted to learn. I wanted to be a good partner—and I liked talking to Rory, even if I wasn't using my voice.

Mostly, our conversing was about our project, but after we'd met a few times I finally found the nerve to ask him why he chose me and not anyone else to be his partner.

"It's a long story," he said, and sighed. "And it doesn't really matter."

The tone of his voice told me that it did matter, but I didn't push him. I, of all people, knew when somebody didn't want to talk.

In addition to these important non-science-related developments, we had made significant strides on our project. We had constructed two different nose cones, a large one and small one, and we had also built several versions of fins, which are the wing things that sit on the bottom of the rocket. The goal was to get your rocket to go as high as possible, and two of the biggest variables impacting its performance were the nose cone and the fins.

It was my idea to build all the different sizes and styles

so we could switch them in and out until we found the combination that made our rocket fly best. Rory thought I was so smart when I first mentioned that, and he thought I was a genius when he saw my notes and sketches of the different prototypes I envisioned.

"Holy cow! Thea, this is incredible! I'm mean the drawings are great, but you could be working for NASA with all of these notes and calculations about the design."

It felt good to hear him say that, but it felt even better to be doing a science project again. Even if this wasn't studying nature, I loved the process. Our work reminded me of how Charlie would test out different lures and stretches of water on Clover Creek until he found what caught the fish. I knew then our rocket was going to soar.

On this particular afternoon, we were ready to test our rocket for the first time. Mr. Morris had a special contraption that he would be using to launch everyone's rocket on the big day, but for our immediate purposes Rory had rigged up our own device, which consisted of a launch pad, cork, and bicycle air pump. (I thought he was the genius after seeing that.) The idea was quite simple: After adding some water, we'd cork the bottle and position it upside down on the launch pad. Then we'd continuously pump air into it, building up pressure until it blew the cork out of the bottom, thus propelling the rocket upward.

Rory got our rocket situated and started filling it with air. I held my breath in anticipation. Waiting. Waiting. Up and down he continued working the handle. How much was it going to take? I began to wonder. And then—bam! All at once our vessel shot off the ground, climbing higher than I ever expected.

"Wow!" Simon cried, craning his neck back to see. "Blamo! Bango! Whamo!" he cheered, dancing in celebration, which had my sisters laughing and Jack running around and barking.

A few seconds later our project came crashing down into their pile of leaves.

"Do it again! Do it again!" Simon shouted, retrieving our rocket and running back to us with it in his hands, Jack-Jack on his heels the whole way. "Do it again, Rory," he insisted.

"Give me a chance, and I will."

I switched out the nose cones and got things hooked up and in position, and then Rory did it again. We conducted a total of ten trials that afternoon, some better than others, but overall it was a great success.

"I know what would help your rocket go even higher," Simon claimed when we were packing up.

"Oh yeah? What's that?" Rory asked him.

"Your rocket needs a name. It's supposed to have a name painted down the side."

"You know what, you're right," Rory said, glancing at me and smirking. "I think we'll call it the *Simonator.*"

"Yeah!" Simon cheered. "The *Simonator!*" He raced around the field with his arms held out like an airplane doing figure eights with sound effects until Jack-Jack bounded over and knocked him to the ground and started tickling him with his nose. Simon's giggles echoed across the schoolyard. I swear, Jack was the only one I knew with more energy than that little boy.

When I looked up, I spotted Ms. Stacy standing off to the side, surveying the scene with a big smile on her face. There was an awful lot for her to be happy about.

40

THANKSGIVING

It was Thanksgiving. In Mom's opinion, the most-special family dinner of the year. Christmas and Easter ranked pretty high, but there were presents and baskets that took away from the significance of the meal. She had a point. At Thanksgiving the focus really was just on the food and—major eye roll—simply being together around the table. Worst of all, my parents liked to add a layer of torture by asking each of us to say what we were thankful for before eating anything.

"I'll go first," Mom said. "I'm thankful for our health and beautiful new home, and I'm especially thankful your father got past his dumb crate idea with Jackson."

On cue, Jack barked. We all jumped and then my sisters and I lost it. We couldn't hold in our giggles, and once we got going it was hard to stop. It wasn't like Mom to make a joke during this tradition, so that just made it even funnier. Add to that the fact that Jack never barked at the table and that made it funnier still. It was like Jack was agreeing with Mom, emphasizing that the crate really was a dumb idea. I glanced down and gave his head a rub.

"Ha, ha," Dad said. "Well, I'm thankful for my own brilliant idea that brought Mr. Jackson into our lives in the first place. But I'm most thankful to see my daughter laughing again—even if it is at my own expense."

That was really sweet, but talk about taking the mood from light and fun to super serious. Jeez, Dad. I was grateful for my sisters after that, because they got us back to light and fun.

"I'm thankful that Jack-Jack is helping Simon so he's not being naughty in school anymore and bothering me or taking my stuff," Abby said.

"I'm thankful for that too, and for Ms. Stacy," Livvy said.

It was my turn. I took a breath. "I'm thankful for my family, and Jack-Jack, and Ms. Stacy," I said, reaching down to give Jack's head another scratch.

"Don't forget Rory," Livvy teased.

"Yeah, and your rocket, 'cause you won," Abby added.

Mom smiled at me from across the table.

"All right," Dad said, "let's dig in while it's still hot."

We began making our plates and passing the food around.

And Rory, I thought. Our rocket did sail higher than any others. And when it finally came back down to earth, I turned and hugged him I was so excited.

"We won," I whispered.

"So that's what your voice sounds like," he said.

And then we ran to fetch our winning rocket—the *Simonator*.

I had much to be thankful for on this Thanksgiving, when I didn't know if I'd ever feel that way again.

PART IV

41

SANTA

What was supposed to be a low-key weekend turned out to be anything but.

Liv and Abby went grocery shopping with Mom so that they could pick out the snacks they wanted for their lunches during the week, and on their way home they heard the now-infamous commercial on the radio. It was an advertisement for family photos with Santa at the local pet store.

"Bring your dog to meet Santa" was all my sisters needed to hear.

Mom agreed it was a great idea because then she could use the photo for our Christmas card this year. Dad and I were filled in on the sudden plans as soon as they got home. So after we got the groceries put away and grabbed some lunch, we donned our ugly sweaters and made the trip to Pete's Pet Supplies.

The line for dogs to meet the big guy wrapped around the store. Jack-Jack sniffed more butts than I could count.

He had fun saying hi and making friends, but eventually he got bored. So did I. I wasn't paying attention when we moved forward and were suddenly standing next to the large bin of tennis balls. And I wasn't paying attention when Jack lifted his leg and peed all over them. By the time I came to my senses and realized what he was doing, it was too late.

What do you do after something like that happens? Do you tell someone or pretend you didn't see it? Remember: Santa's watching.

That was a tough one, made much easier because I had a little sister. Once Abby spotted Jack-Jack's yellow puddle of urine spreading across the floor she hurried and told the nearest store employee, a purple-haired guy who, according to his badge, happened to be named Thor.

"No sweat," Thor said when Abby showed him the accident. "Believe you me, your dog's not the first to give that bin of tennis balls a good spritz, but most people pretend they didn't see it and never tell us, so thanks for letting me know, little Wonder Woman."

Abby beamed at the praise and Thor gave her a fist bump.

"Let me get my supplies and I'll clean it up," he said.

A few minutes later Thor returned with a roll of paper towels and disinfectant spray. It didn't take long before he had the hazardous area wiped up and then Jack-Jack ventured over and nosed his hand. I think he was trying to apologize. Thor patted Jack on the head and then he reached into his pocket and pulled out a cookie. Judging by the fierce tail wagging and excited body shaking, the treat was very much appreciated. Jack-Jack liked Thor—but he had an entirely different reaction to the guy waiting for him at the end of the line.

You could chalk this up to another idea that sounded great in theory but was an utter disaster in reality. I should have known. At least Dad could say this one wasn't his fault.

42

THE MILLION-DOLLAR QUESTION

"Hello, Thea," Ms. Stacy said when I walked into her classroom on Monday afternoon. "How was your weekend?"

I snorted. "Embarrassing. Hilarious. Unforgettable. Take your pick, but I don't know if there is a word to describe it."

"Oh boy. What did Jack do this time?"

We sat down in our usual seats and I started from the beginning, telling her all about our trip to see Santa. I told her about the tennis balls and Thor and all the dogs, before getting to the best part.

"So we waited in line for about fifty minutes, and then it was finally our turn," I continued. "Two employees, both dressed as elves, came to greet us. One showed us where to stand while the other took Jack's leash and guided him over to Santa. Everything was fine until the elf tried to hoist Jack off the ground and place him on Santa's lap."

"Oh no," Ms. Stacy said.

"'Oh no' is right. Jack freaked when he got a close-up of the bearded man in the red suit. Santa was no match for my terrified dog. Jack broke free from Santa's grasp and lunged off his lap, knocking the big man to the ground. The guy's hat went flying and his beard and glasses were twisted sideways."

Ms. Stacy gasped.

"His two elves, being dedicated good helpers, attempted to stop Jack. That didn't go well either. He bowled them over and dashed for the door. Luckily, Thor was there to greet Jack-Jack and calmly took his leash and led him outside."

Ms. Stacy sat with her hand covering her mouth, shaking her head in disbelief. I kept going.

"Dad rushed to help Santa back to his bench while Mom hurried to give the elves a hand. My parents were mortified. Meanwhile, Abby and I ran to find Thor and Jack-Jack. Livvy was with us, but the cameraman stopped her just long enough to give her our Polaroid. He'd captured an epic action shot of our family."

I slid the picture in front of Ms. Stacy.

"Oh my goodness," she whispered. "This is priceless."

"I know. I actually think it rivals Charlie's Santa photo for best ever."

"Charlie had a Santa photo of this caliber?" Ms. Stacy asked.

"He sure did," I said. "It was taken when he was a toddler. I wasn't there of course, but you know what they say, a picture's worth a thousand words."

"Case in point," Ms. Stacy agreed, raising Jack's Polaroid as proof.

I smiled and continued with Charlie's story. "So I guess the elves stuck Charlie on Santa's lap, and just like Jack, Charlie had a freak-out. He chomped down on Santa's thumb, and the moment the man's grip loosened, Charlie scooted from his lap and streaked past the elf. In Charlie's photo, you see Santa with his mouth wide open, howling in obvious pain and shaking his freshly bitten hand, and Charlie's backside as he's beginning his getaway."

Ms. Stacy snickered.

"I know. Every time I looked at that picture I'd laugh, so Charlie finally gave it to me for my Christmas present last year. He stuck it in the middle of a homemade card where he'd drawn a picture of Santa wearing swim trunks and a snorkel mask and flippers. Charlie might've been the only kid in the whole world who didn't like Santa Claus."

We laughed, and then . . .

"Thea, what happened to Charlie?"

43

I TELL THE STORY

My breath caught. There it was. The million-dollar question. She'd finally asked it. I didn't realize it then, but Ms. Stacy wasn't asking for herself. She was asking because she knew I wanted to tell her. I needed to tell someone.

I stared at my desk. Slowly, I inhaled and exhaled, and then I began. "It was before we moved here. Charlie and I were on our way home from Clover Creek. It was nearing dusk and fog had moved in . . . We'd stayed longer than we should've, but that was because we were having a great time. Charlie had taught me how to fish and I caught my first rainbow trout that afternoon." I looked up and smiled at the memory. "I was so excited—Charlie too."

My smile faded and my gaze returned to the desk in front of me. "We texted our parents to let them know we were on our way back. The creek wasn't that far from home . . . everything was supposed to be fine. We were walking along the side of the road, chatting away, when a doe and her fawn came out of the woods and started to cross just ahead of us."

I stopped, taking a minute to ready myself before continuing with what happened next. Ms. Stacy waited.

I took another breath and then I kept going. "I gasped and the deer heard me and froze. We stood perfectly still, Charlie and me grasping hands and watching the incredible scene, and the mother and baby deer staring back at us." I swallowed. "The black SUV came around the bend so suddenly . . . headlights blaring . . . with nowhere to go. The driver swerved to miss the deer . . . I can still feel the metal brushing past, ripping Charlie's hand from mine and tossing his body through the air."

Ms. Stacy looked like the deer caught in headlights now. "Charlie was hit and killed by a black SUV?" she asked, wide-eyed, her voice shaking.

I nodded.

She sprung from her chair as if shot from a cannon. In a rush, Ms. Stacy grabbed her coat and purse from the closet. Then she took everything that was sitting on top of her desk and crammed it into her school bag. "I just remembered. I have an appointment."

I'd never seen her like this. Completely flustered. Face flushed. Keeping her eyes from mine.

"Pull the door closed behind you," she said.

And then she was gone.

44

TURNING UGLY

I was at Arena Elementary the next day after school, and the next, but Ms. Stacy was not. I stood in her doorway, wondering where she could've gone. I'd been patient, but now I was growing frustrated. It hadn't been easy for me to tell her what had happened. And she responded by disappearing? I thought she cared about me, but apparently, I was wrong. On second thought, I was past frustrated. I was angry.

"Mom hasn't seen or heard from her, either," Rory said when he came around the corner and saw me standing there. "It's not like her. Do you know anything?"

I could have said that I'd told her about Charlie's accident, and that she'd run off. I could have simply said that I didn't know. I could have shrugged my shoulders and said nothing, but I didn't do any of those things. Instead, I turned ugly. "What do you care?" I snapped.

Rory's face registered shock.

"Well?" I growled.

"I . . . I was just asking because Mom says Simon isn't handling her absence well," he barely uttered, his voice disappearing by the end.

Liv and Abby had said the same. Simon just wasn't himself without Ms. Stacy, but I still brought Jack-Jack with me. The least I could do was keep that part of his life steady, even if he wasn't technically earning his reward. Even if his teacher wasn't holding up her end of the bargain.

Ms. Stacy was letting all of us down, and that thought took me from ugly to mean. None of this was Rory's fault, but I unloaded on him. "You act like you care, but you don't," I snarled. "You think you're something special with your fancy sign language, but you're not. It's dumb. Why don't you go back to your bulletin boards?"

Rory swallowed. The look on his face tore me up inside. "You know what, I liked you a whole lot better when you didn't say a word." He shook his head. "You're the one who doesn't care. You don't know me or anything about me."

He turned and walked away, and I was left standing there—just me and my ugly mean self.

Rory was right. I didn't know him. It was obvious that I'd hurt him—but I was so mad that I told myself it was true that I didn't care.

45

THE STRANGER

It was another two days before Ms. Stacy finally returned and I got answers.

"Thea, I want to apologize for leaving in such a rush the last time we were together," she said, taking her usual seat across from me.

"You had an appointment," I reminded her, pulling in my chair.

"No, that was my excuse," she confessed, looking me in the eye. "Thea, when you told me what happened to Charlie . . . it was just so hard to believe. I wasn't expecting—"

"It's all right," I said, trying to make her feel better.

"No, you don't understand."

My face scrunched.

"Thea, there's somebody I think you should meet."

I stiffened. What did she mean? Ms. Stacy was the only one I talked to about this stuff. I didn't want to meet a stranger. But whoever she had in mind was already there.

Ms. Stacy rose from her chair and stepped out of the classroom. I stood up. I thought about bolting, but there was no time for me to escape. She was back within a few seconds.

"Thea, this is my brother, Hank," Ms. Stacy said, introducing me to the gentleman by her side.

I did one of those forced cheek-smiles and her brother did the same. I don't know if he looked away first or if it was me, but before we did our eyes met, just for an instant, but it was enough.

My legs buckled under me. I had to grab on to the desk to keep from falling. Ms. Stacy was still talking, but I wasn't hearing anything she said. I couldn't breathe.

Hank's eyes—red and full of anguish—were the same ones that had stared back at me when he knelt next to Charlie's limp body.

I couldn't believe this was happening. I ran—just like I did after the accident. I ran down the hall, around the corner, and burst out the doors.

"Thea!" Ms. Stacy called after me. "Thea!"

I never stopped.

46

A KNOCK ON OUR DOOR

Even after the terrible things I'd said and the horrible way I'd treated him, Rory still walked home with my sisters and Jack-Jack after he'd seen me running away. Actions speak louder than words, and Rory had just shown he was a much better person than me.

"Call me if you need anything," I heard him telling my sisters before leaving, which just made me squeeze my pillow and cry harder.

Jack came to my bedroom straightaway and stayed with me, while Liv and Abby left me alone, which made me wonder what else Rory had said to them. My sisters even tried to carry on like normal at dinner that night, pretending everything was fine, but I wasn't doing a good job playing my part. I was always quiet, but tonight I was distant. Mom did her best to act like she was listening to Liv and Abby; ever since the mystery box she made sure to pay attention, but I saw her exchange pointed looks with Dad. Something was up.

"Everything all right, Thea?" Dad finally asked. "You haven't eaten a thing, and you're just pushing your food around your plate."

Mom turned her attention to me. Here come the twenty questions, I thought. Not that I'd answer any of them, but Mom couldn't help being concerned. Fortunately, it didn't come to any of that. Instead, there was an unexpected knock on our door.

I stiffened and Jack-Jack perked up next to my chair.

Mom rose from the table and went to see who it was. She peeked out the window before opening the door. "Oh, it's Ms. Stacy," she announced.

"Ms. Stacy!" my sisters cheered, leaving their chairs and running to greet their teacher.

I was gone in a flash, racing to my bedroom, Jack on my heels. I sat on my bed, knees pulled close to my chest, my back pressed against the wall. Jack-Jack rested his head on my hip and I rubbed his ears. We stayed there, waiting. No doubt, my parents would be coming to check on me after Ms. Stacy left.

I was wrong. So wrong.

47

HURT TOGETHER, HEAL TOGETHER

It was Ms. Stacy, not Mom or Dad, who came to my room. She knocked lightly and stepped inside. Jack's tail thumped against the mattress.

"Hi, Jack-Jack," she whispered, walking over and petting him. She took a seat on the edge of my bed. "Thea, I'm sorry. After you ran, I realized that I'd gotten ahead of myself and I felt terrible. I still feel terrible. I called your parents and told them what happened and asked if I could come by tonight. I should've talked to them first; I should've asked you first, or found a gentler way to tell you. It's just . . . I've seen my brother hurting for a long time now . . . and you as well. And I think the two of you can help each other, if you talk. That's all. I'm sorry."

Silent tears fell from my cheeks. I tried pulling Jack close, but he wiggled free from my grasp and jumped to the floor. He'd never left my side, especially when I was upset. But he walked to my doorway and stopped. He stood there, tail pointed, body erect, staring into the hallway and sniffing the air. And then he started whining and whimpering.

"Oh my gosh. Hey there, little fella," said a voice outside my bedroom. Hank came into view when he bent down to pet my dog. Jack's tail wagged like it did for me, his body shaking with excitement. He stood on his hind legs and stretched to kiss Hank's face.

Hank chuckled. "It's good to see you too, buddy. I'm sure glad things worked out for you."

"Hank, do you know this dog?" Ms. Stacy asked.

Hank hugged Jack-Jack and looked over at us. "I sure do. I saved him," he replied.

Rebecca's words came rushing back to me. *Jack was abandoned at a very young age. And probably because of his lazy eye. But luckily, someone with a good heart stumbled upon him before it was too late.*

"You're the one who found him?" I croaked.

Hank nodded.

I swallowed, fighting the knot in my throat. What were the chances? The same man who'd hit and killed Charlie . . . had saved Jack-Jack.

"I did all I could, Thea," he rasped. "I knelt by Charlie's side, holding him. I kept talking to him until the ambulance came, begging him to be okay. I tried so hard. And I'm so sorry."

Hank's voice cracked and then he broke down, burying his face in his hands and sobbing. I'd never seen a grown man cry like that.

Jack-Jack rooted at Hank's hands, pushing them out of the way so that he could get to his face and lick the tears.

I don't know where I found the courage—I think it was in trusting Jack-Jack; he was telling me it was okay same as he'd found a way to tell me it was okay to go for a walk, to hide dog poop in Abby's mystery box, to part with Roscoe, and so many other things—but I slid off my bed and walked across my bedroom and knelt next to Hank. "I'm sorry I ran," I said, my voice barely above a whisper. "I was so scared . . . I knew it was bad but I didn't know what to do. I panicked . . . and then I ran to get my parents."

Hank rubbed his eyes. "You don't need to be sorry, Thea. None of this was your fault."

He wasn't the first to tell me that, but it felt different coming from him. Fresh tears streamed down my cheeks, falling and landing on my thighs. "I can't help thinking it should've been me," I choked.

"That wouldn't make it any better. Charlie would be here missing you just the same. And I . . ." He couldn't finish.

I sniffled. Then I lifted my chin and looked at him. "It's not your fault, either," I said. "It was foggy and I know you didn't see us. You only saw the deer."

I heard Ms. Stacy's breath catch. I glanced over and saw her cover her mouth, her eyes welling with tears.

Hank's jaw trembled. I knew the pain in his face

mirrored my own. Slowly, we leaned across the space between us and hugged, squeezing our arms tight, Jack-Jack sandwiched between us.

I'm not sure how long my parents stood in the hallway before coming into my bedroom, but they were by my side after that. "We love you," Mom whispered, pulling me close.

Dad kissed the top of my head. "We love you, honey."

An emotional Ms. Stacy joined us on the floor next and held her brother.

Hank and I hurt together and healed together on that night. He was the same man who'd hit and killed Charlie and also saved Jack-Jack. And now our paths were crossing these many months later. There was mystery in that. I think I knew then, but I still wasn't there yet. I wanted to see it as coincidence. That was easier. I wasn't ready to believe something bigger.

48

THE HARDWARE STORE

"I need to make a trip to the hardware store," Dad announced during breakfast a few days later. "The weather forecast has us getting our first big snowfall this week, and I need a new shovel. My old one broke during the move."

"Can you get some ice melt while you're there?" Mom asked.

"The pet-safe kind," I added, scratching Jack-Jack's head.

"Why don't you and Jack come with me," Dad suggested. "The two of you can pick out the type you want."

I looked at Jack and shrugged. "Want to go for a ride?"

I no sooner got the word "ride" out of my mouth than he sprang to his feet and trotted to the door. He looked back at us, tail wagging.

"Yup, he wants to go," Abby said.

We all laughed.

So it was shortly after breakfast when Jack and I

climbed into the car with Dad and made the trip. Jack enjoyed the ride with his head hanging out the back window, but the store was even better. His nose was working nonstop from the moment we got inside. There was so much he had to smell. But don't worry, after his incident with the tennis balls, I knew to pay attention. He thought about peeing on the wheels of one snow blower, and he tried to grab a pair of winter gloves off the shelf, but I stopped him both times.

It didn't take long. We picked out the right ice melt and Dad got his shovel. Jack had his fun, but you could say the visit to the store itself was rather uneventful—which I'll admit was probably better than another pet-store disaster. It was what happened in the parking lot that was important.

Jack-Jack and I climbed into the car while Dad loaded our purchases in the trunk. I had just buckled my seat belt when Jack started barking in the back seat.

"What is it, boy?" I asked, glancing out the window to see what had him so excited.

It was Rory. The second I spotted him across the parking lot, I began hurting. He was with a man and they were using sign language.

Jack continued to bark until Rory looked in our direction, and the instant he did Jack's barking turned into whimpering. Rory saw us. He saw me. His eyes met mine, but he didn't wave—and neither did I. Instead, I watched his shoulders sag as he turned away from us. The man with him never looked in our direction.

Dad opened his door and sat behind the wheel. "What was all that barking about?" he asked.

I shrugged, pretending I didn't know, and glanced back at Jack-Jack. He whimpered a few more times before growing quiet. I understood. I felt the same way. And it wasn't going to get any better until I did something about it.

49

I'M SORRY

Ms. Stacy was in her classroom, but it was Rory I needed to talk to . . . if he'd let me. I'd waited until now because there was no way I was trying this at the middle school with other kids around. Jack-Jack was off having fun with my sisters and Simon, so this was my chance. I knew where to find him.

"Can I give you a hand?" I asked, approaching the bulletin board where he was busy replacing turkeys with snowmen.

He shrugged.

I glanced around and spotted an extra staple remover in the bin on the floor. I grabbed it and began taking turkeys down, careful not to damage them because I saw that Rory was keeping them, probably for next year.

"Thank you for walking my sisters and Jack-Jack home the other day," I said, tossing a handful of staples into the trash.

He nodded.

"That was really nice of you . . . especially after the way I treated you," I admitted, my voice fading.

He shrugged again.

Usually I was the one not talking, but our roles had reversed, which wasn't making this very easy. You could say I was getting a taste of my own medicine—but I deserved it.

"Did you say anything to Ms. Stacy about me getting upset?" I asked, trying to get more out of him. His silence was uncomfortable. I bent down and put my turkeys inside their designated folder, waiting to see if he'd respond. Finally, he did.

Rory sighed. "After I walked your sisters and Jack home and came back here, I saw Ms. Stacy. I asked her if you were okay . . . and then I told her about what had happened."

"And what did she say?" How much did Rory know? I wondered.

"Only that I need to forgive you . . . and that I definitely shouldn't believe what you said because it came from a place of deep pain."

"She's right. About not believing any of what I said," I quickly clarified, "because I didn't mean any of those things. . . . But I don't blame you if you can't forgive me."

Rory looked at me then.

"I'm sorry," I croaked. "Truly sorry."

"I know."

"You do?" I asked, feeling relief.

"Yeah, I do. My dad has mastered reading lips, but I've gotten pretty good at reading people."

I swallowed. "Was that who I saw you with, outside the hardware store?"

He nodded.

I bit my lip, wanting to ask more, but not sure if I should, so I returned to the bulletin board. I took a snowman and handed it to Rory. I watched him attach it and then I gave him another.

"Has he always been deaf? Your father, I mean," I finally managed.

"Took you long enough," Rory replied.

My mouth fell open. "You knew I was struggling with that question the whole time and didn't say anything? Ugh," I groaned, and shoved him.

"Told you I could read people," he said, and laughed.

I stuck my tongue out at him and sneered, but then broke into a smile—one that he returned.

"My dad lost his hearing last year," Rory said after we got done fooling around.

I felt a sharp pang of guilt. I didn't know what to say.

"He got sick and ended up in the hospital with some sort of infection, a virus or something that the doctors couldn't explain. They don't know if it was the virus or the high doses of medicine they were giving him that took his hearing, but it was a big shock."

I handed him the last snowman. "That must've been hard."

"It was," he acknowledged. "For Mom. For me. But especially for my dad."

"I'm sorry."

Rory attached the final snowman and then looked at me again. "It's okay. Anyway, that's why I know sign language."

"Which is very cool, by the way, and not dumb like I said."

He grinned and then I did the sign for "thank you."

He replied with "you're welcome."

Our moment of quiet ended there because just then there was a burst of commotion coming from the entrance. Simon came running, my sisters and Jack-Jack not far behind.

"Hey, are those snowmen sledding?" Simon yelled when he saw the new bulletin board.

Rory grinned. "Yup."

"What're you guys doing inside?" I asked.

"Simon's gotta pee," Abby announced.

Judging by the way Simon was holding himself and dancing in place, it looked like he had to go pretty bad, but he couldn't stop staring at Rory's bulletin board. "I've never been sledding on a big hill like that," he said.

"You haven't?" Rory asked.

"Nope. Just down the small one behind my house, and it's not very good."

"We've gotta fix that, then," Rory said. "Tell you what, when our first snow comes, I'll take you sledding on a big hill."

"You will?" Simon squealed.

"Promise," Rory said.

"Can we come too?" Abby asked.

Rory glanced at me. "Yeah, we can all go," he said, and smiled.

I still hadn't told Rory my story, and I was sure there was more to his, but we'd fill in the gaps with time. I knew because I felt lighter and better when I was with him—and maybe some other feelings too.

50

PERFECT CONDITIONS

It was a perfect afternoon for sledding. School had let out early because teachers were having a meeting, and since Christmas break was right around the corner there wasn't any homework or projects I had to worry about, and on top of that, the conditions were just right—it was cold, with temperatures in the twenties but no real wind-chill, and the sun was shining bright. We'd gotten two more inches of fresh powder overnight, but sitting beneath that was the best packing snow. Blazing the first trail wouldn't be fun because the fluffy stuff resting on top was sure to blow in our faces, but once we got past that it would be smooth sailing—or, according to Rory, speed racing. He was taking us to the notorious Thatcher's Hill. "Us" being my sisters and Simon and me, and Jack-Jack, of course.

Jack and I met all of them on the corner when Arena Elementary dismissed. The plan was simple: Walk to our house so my sisters and Simon could drop off their backpacks and Liv and Abby and I could grab our sleds. Simon and Rory already had their sleds with them.

We skipped along Salem Street, my sisters taking advantage of the bright sun behind us to play shadow tag, and Simon asking Rory a million questions about Thatcher's Hill. Rory was the only one of us who'd been there before. Simon had heard stories about it but never had anyone to take him there. His parents were more than happy to let him tag along with us today, because then they didn't have to worry about getting out of work early to pick him up from school.

My sisters and I listened as Rory described the hill. "It's so steep there've been snowmobiles that couldn't make it to the top. Some people estimate you reach speeds close to twenty or thirty miles per hour when you go zipping down it. They say one person went so fast the bottom of their sled melted right under their butt."

"Whoa!" Simon cried. The boy couldn't contain his energy and excitement on a regular basis, so add the legend of Thatcher's Hill to the mix and you had a kid jumping and spinning and karate-kicking out of control. Rory's tall tales coupled with Simon's enthusiasm were amusing until Simon stumbled and dropped his sled.

We had just made it to the top of the one and only hill we needed to climb on the way to our house when it happened. Simon's sled hit the sidewalk and skidded backwards, gaining speed as it continued down the slope before veering into Salem Street.

Everyone has heard stories about little kids chasing

their ball into the road. Every parent tells those stories as a way to warn their own child not to do it. I used to wonder if any of those tales were true. They were now.

"No!" Simon yelled, chasing after his sled.

I felt the leash yank and then go limp. Jack lunged so hard that he broke his collar.

I can't describe much of what took place after that moment because I couldn't see. The sun glare blinded me. Luckily, the driver of the large truck rumbling up the hill had the sun at his back, and could see. He swerved to miss Simon, and when he did the wagon load of hay he had in tow jackknifed right in the middle of Salem Street, sending hay bales flying and snow clouds and straw everywhere. Brakes screeched, horns blared, and voices cried out from every direction. When the dust finally settled there were people everywhere.

Simon lay sprawled out in the snowbank on the other side of the road. At first glance, I knew he was all right because his body didn't have the same awkward angle that Charlie's had, but we still ran to check on him, and breathed sighs of relief when we saw he was unharmed. The man who'd been driving the hay truck and the drivers of other cars in the vicinity weren't far behind us. They all stopped and got out and rushed to check on Simon as well.

But where was Jack? Frantically, I searched up and down Salem Street. No sign of him. With my heart in my throat, I asked Rory to check under the hay wagon. I couldn't look.

Tentatively, Rory knelt and peered underneath. "He's not here."

I let out the breath I'd been holding.

Rory straightened. "There's no sign of him anywhere."

"He hates large trucks and loud engines. I still can't believe he ran toward it," I said.

"He saved Simon. The truck driver said he saw Jack knock Simon out of the way, but he didn't see where he went after that."

"Maybe he got scared and ran off?" Livvy suggested. "If he did, he'll find his way home."

I nodded, but somehow I knew that wasn't going to be the case. Hard to explain, but I felt it. For the past three days, when I awoke in the morning Jack hadn't been in bed with me. It was as if he was preparing me for this. These were perfect conditions . . . perfect for Jack-Jack to disappear.

"You kids have sure got one special dog there," the truck driver said, coming over to us. "How he escaped my tires, I'll never know."

"He's Houdini Dog," Abby responded.

"He vanished, all right," the driver replied. "A real mystery."

He was that—and so much more.

51

SEARCHING

The mere hope that Jack-Jack would be waiting for us on the front doorstep when we got home was what helped Liv and Abby hold it together. It was also the reason we slipped away from the commotion surrounding the scene on Salem Street as fast as we could. Like Jack, we disappeared before anyone noticed. But when we walked up to the house, there was no sign of our beloved dog.

"Where is he?" Abby cried.

"Jack-Jack!" Livvy yelled.

"Here, boy!" I shouted.

"Jack!" Rory and Simon hollered.

After calling him for a solid minute, we held our breaths and stood silent, waiting. Praying. When he didn't come, we tried again. When there was still no sign of him, my sisters grew even more anxious.

"Where is he?" Abby whined.

"Maybe he's lost," Simon suggested.

"We've got to go looking for him!" Abby shrieked.

"We need to hang up posters on all the trees and telephone poles," Livvy said, thinking strategically.

"Yeah, lost-dog posters," Simon agreed. "With a ten thousand-dollar reward!"

I didn't have the strength or heart to tell my sisters it would never work. Jack-Jack wasn't lost. I knew it in my bones. He'd found my sisters on the first day he escaped his crate. He could find us now if he wanted.

"Good idea," Rory said, speaking up for me since I was lost in my own thoughts.

We went inside and Rory helped my sisters and Simon get started on the posters while I called Mom. Rory was smart and convinced them to change the ten-thousand-dollar part to just REWARD, so then we weren't obligated to pay a certain amount.

Both Mom and Dad left work and got home as fast as they could after hearing the news. We took the posters and made over a hundred copies. Then we drove around the neighborhood hanging them up and searching for Jack-Jack.

We searched high and low. Dad drove around for hours and hours every morning and night for a week. Rory's mom even put a note in her principal newsletter. And when Christmas break came, we hung up new signs and drove around even more.

We never found him. We never would.

52

CHRISTMAS EVE DINNER

We sat around the dinner table on Christmas Eve, excited for Christmas Day, but still struggling to find normal again in the absence of Jack. We'd gone from talking about him and the possibility of finding him, to not mentioning his name at all—a clear sign that we'd lost hope—until Abby accidentally dropped her meatball on the floor.

"Now's when we need Jackson," Dad said. "He'd clean that up in no time."

At first, I thought that was a slip. But it wasn't. Dad knew what he was doing.

"What do you think happened to him?" Livvy asked. "I keep thinking about him being lost and all alone again, like when he was a puppy, and it makes me sad."

"Me too," Abby followed. "I miss him."

"He's not lost," I said with no uncertainty.

"Where did he go?" Abby asked.

I took a moment before answering. It can be hard to open up and share what you hold close, even with family, sometimes more with family, but I found the courage for my sisters, hoping it might bring them some comfort. "I don't know where he's gone," I admitted, "but I know he's safe and happy."

"How do you know?" Abby pressed, a scowl creasing her forehead.

"Jack-Jack was special," I said, "but more than your normal special. He came into our lives when I needed him most. So many things happened in the last few months . . . because of him."

"He gave us our big sister back," Livvy said.

I smiled.

"And my daughter," Mom choked, reaching across the table and taking my hand.

Dad took my other hand. "Jack's work here was done, so it was time for him to move on," he explained to my sisters.

"Do you think Jack-Jack was an angel?" Livvy asked.

Dad squeezed my hand. Mom too.

I swallowed. "I think he was Charlie."

53

MERRY CHRISTMAS

We gathered in the living room on Christmas morning. Mom passed out our presents and we took turns opening them. It was a happy celebration, mixed with a tinge of sadness. It was time for us to move on, but that didn't mean we weren't still missing Jack, especially after seeing his unopened package sitting under the tree by its lonesome.

We were on our last gifts when we were interrupted. The knock on our door was unexpected, but the surprise on the other side was perfect timing.

"Who in the heavens could that be knocking on our door on Christmas morning?" Mom said to no one in particular. She sighed in exasperation as she got to her feet and went to check.

The rest of us sat and waited for her to return before continuing with the unwrapping.

"Oh my goodness!" Mom exclaimed after peeking through the window to see who it was.

"What?" my sisters chorused.

Mom pulled open the door and there stood Rory and Simon and Ms. Stacy. And resting in Simon's arms was just what we needed.

"We brought you a present," Simon announced, marching into our house. "Merry Christmas!"

My sisters squealed.

"We wanted to do something for your family," Ms. Stacy said to Mom. "I hope this is okay."

Mom glanced at my sisters, who were on the floor, giggling and playing with the puppy. "It's just what we needed," she said. "Thank you."

I got up and hugged Ms. Stacy first, and then Rory. "Thank you," I whispered.

Rory smiled and my insides turned all funny feeling.

"Don't worry, Mr. Ettinger, we picked out a boy dog," Rory said.

Dad laughed. He liked Rory too.

"I'm sorry about Jack-Jack," Simon told us. "I miss him."

"We all miss him," Mom said, "but we'll always remember him."

"Jack-Jack saved me," Simon replied.

"He saved me too," I said.

Simon smiled and then Rory and I got down on the floor with my sisters and him to see the new puppy.

WHAT COMES NEXT

MONTHS LATER

Mom was right. We were okay. Our new puppy was doing a great job of keeping us entertained and on our toes—turns out, he liked Dad's shoes even more than Jack-Jack had. On the bright side, he also didn't have an issue with the crate, so that part of training was *much* easier. And Simon found getting to play with him in the afternoons to be just as motivating, so he continued to do better for Ms. Stacy and his classmates—meaning Liv and Abby.

As far as middle school goes, not much changed. I wasn't scared to talk if called on, but I also didn't go out of my way to strike up conversations with people—other than Rory—although there was one exception. I didn't plan it. It just sort of happened.

Rory and I were sitting at lunch, discussing our new science assignment. (Forgot to mention, I didn't need to hide in the bathroom anymore, either.) We were studying ecosystems in class and Mr. Morris wanted us to write about one that was important to us and tell why. I was excited because this was right up my alley. I was thinking about choosing Whitman Forest and was showing Rory some of the sketches and notes I had from my previous visits there.

"Thea, this is like *National Geographic* stuff," he said.

I grinned. "I actually think I'd like to work for them one day."

"If they saw this, they'd hire you now!" he exclaimed.

I laughed. "You're nuts."

"I'm serious," he said, then laughed with me.

I put my journal away and took another bite of my sandwich. I was chewing when she came walking by our table.

"Hi, Ms. Riley," Rory said.

"Hi, Rory," she replied.

It was simple as that.

I swallowed. "You know her?" I asked him.

"Yeah, she helped me through some rough times."

"You mean after your dad lost his hearing?"

He nodded. "A lot of people were eager to help, and they did for a while, but Ms. Riley stuck by my side for the long haul. It took months before my dad could go back to work—and he got depressed. My mom was struggling too. And me. I had to quit running track because it was just too much. There were so many changes to figure out for our family, and Mom needed my help."

"Wow, that stinks. I'm sorry."

"That's how I ended up doing the bulletin boards and spending so much time at Arena Elementary. But I plan on running again this spring, because things are better now. It was hard when it was all happening, though. Ms. Riley was always there for me to talk to when I needed her."

"She sounds great," I croaked.

"She is," Rory replied.

When school finished that afternoon, I did something I never thought I'd do again. I walked into Ms. Riley's office.

"Hi, Ms. Riley."

She looked up from her computer.

"I don't know if you remember me, but—"

"I do. Hi, Thea. How are you?"

"Um . . . good, thanks. Anyways, I just wanted to say sorry about everything that happened at the beginning of the year. And I wanted to let you know that I found somebody I could to talk to about that stuff you saw in my file, and you were right, it helped."

"I'm really happy to hear that," she said.

I glanced over my shoulder when I noticed Ms. Riley's gaze moving toward the door. Rory had popped his head in. He was waiting to walk home with me to get our new pup before going to the elementary school.

"Well, I better get going," I said. "Have a nice day, Ms. Riley."

"Thea," she called, stopping me before I was gone. "I'm glad you two found each other."

Wait. No. Did she think Rory was the one I'd found to talk to? . . . Was he?

I smiled and waved. Maybe he was.

YEARS LATER

It was many years before I was ready to revisit Charlie's grave. I wanted him to meet my fiancé. And Rory wanted to meet him. It took me a while, but over time I had told Rory all about Charlie.

However, first things first. I decided we should stop in to see Mr. and Mrs. Gabriel on our way to the cemetery. They had told me long ago that they'd like that. Besides, I wanted to introduce them to Rory as well.

We were all crying in a matter of minutes—Charlie's mom and dad and me—but it was so nice to see them. They were old now, but they were very happy that I'd come. And they just adored Rory.

The four of us sat together drinking iced tea and eating Mrs. Gabriel's fresh apple pie—she was back to baking!— while I brought them up to speed on my life. When we finally got ready to leave for the cemetery, they insisted on coming with us. They visited Charlie every day and hadn't made the trip yet.

His headstone was the same as I remembered it, only weathered, and there was grass where I'd last seen fresh earth. Resting beside him was a new stone—one for a dog. A dog that had shown up on the Gabriels' porch many years ago. A white pup with a brindle patch.

"And if you can believe it," Mrs. Gabriel said, "he had—"

"A lazy eye," I finished.

"It sounds crazy, but that's right. How'd you know?"

"It doesn't sound crazy at all," I said.

Rory squeezed my hand.

I stared at the headstones, side by side, and silently thanked Charlie and the dog I had called Jack for being two of my best friends and favorite beings—one and the same. Just as he'd always wanted to, Charlie had accomplished something special.

How lucky was I to have known them both.

ACKNOWLEDGMENTS

This book would not exist if it weren't for my amazing editor, Françoise Bui. Your patience and encouragement—especially with my early drafts—helped me find Thea's voice and the best way to tell her story. I could not do this without your keen insights and feedback. I'm lucky and beyond grateful that I get to work with you. Thank you so much!

My eternal gratitude to Beverly Horowitz and Paul Fedorko, two people who've stuck with me from the beginning. Your support means everything. And thanks to the entire publishing team at Random House Children's Books. The attention and care you give to my work is so appreciated.

Huge hugs and thanks to my family. Lily and Anya, for always cheering me on and offering advice when it comes to finding the best word or phrase. Thank you to Beth and Emma for reading my first complete draft and providing me with important and thoughtful comments—

even if I didn't always like it. And an extra thanks to Beth for suggesting the title—though I don't remember this, I'll believe you—and for your "what if" during a very important brainstorming session that got me super excited about this story and resulted in one of my favorite connections in the book. Love you all!

And finally, a special mention goes to my rescue dog, Jack, who first inspired this story idea. His miserable performance with the crate and his strong fear of loud trucks got me thinking about his mysterious and complicated past, ultimately leading me to Thea. We've come a long way, bud.

ABOUT THE AUTHOR

Rob Buyea is a former teacher and the author of the Mr. Terupt series and The Perfect Score series. His life has been enriched by numerous dogs since he was a boy. He lives in Massachusetts with his wife, daughters, and two rescue pups.

robbuyea.com